Deadly Deception

Book 2 of the Deception Series

by London St. Charles

LS Charles Publishing Group

Chicago, Illinois

LS Charles Publishing Group
www.londonstcharles.com

Deadly Deception by London St. Charles Copyright ©2020
Trade Paperback ISBN: 978-0-9993288-9-7
E-Book ISBN: 978-0-9993288-7-3

Cover Designed and Interior by:
Gisele Marie: www.authorgiselemarie.com

Dedication

To Shanda, my best friend of thirty-plus years, who has begged me to write a follow-up to *Sugarcoated Deception* ever since she read it while waiting in lines at Great America. I was given orders to hurry up and finish writing "her" book. Here you go, bestie. Enjoy!

Acknowledgements

I started writing this book right after *Sugarcoated Deception* dropped, January 2019, and didn't touch it again until February 2020. I had three other projects in the works, and they consumed my time. As a result, *Deadly Deception* found a temporary home in my 'Manuscripts in Progress' folder. Once I started writing this story again, I fell in love with it. Every detail. Every plot twist. Every tearjerker. I wrote for three weeks straight, starting before work, during the daycare children's nap time, and after they left for the day. Then, the country went on quarantine. For four weeks, half of the people in my household were sick, me being one of them. All writing ceased as I/we recovered. Thank you to those who knew, who reached out, who said prayers, who brought things I needed, and left them at my front door. God is so good. That being said, let me get to it.

Praises to the Almighty for giving me the gift to create and the ability to use it, through Him all things are possible. Thanks for covering my family during this pandemic.

Charles, you're the man! My number one. I couldn't ask for a better husband. If I did, the Lord would send you back to me reincarnated. We were destined.

Mom, here's the rest of your story. You always said it should have been longer. #wink

Sierra & Carrington, I leave you my legacy. I know you don't see it now, but you will. It'll make you appreciate the times I sat at the computer 'ignoring you' lol. Smooches xoxo

Shanda, you recheck the dedication page lol. Love you, Chica.

Christine, Gwen, Marva, Sharon, and Deb, aka my beta readers for this book. Each one of you brings something different to the table. I appreciate your time and feedback.

Gwen, I love the covers for the Deception Series. I told you what I wanted, and boom baby, you made it happen.

The Readers, I hope to keep putting out books that you enjoy and want to tell your family, friends, and co-workers about. Thanks for the continued support.

Until the next story ...

One Love,

London St. Charles

About The Author

National Bestselling Author, **London St. Charles** has always had a passion for the pen, paper, and books. She is a Chicago native who uses the Windy City as a backdrop to the interracial romance, suspense, and contemporary fiction stories she writes. London has contributed to two anthologies, *Sugar* and *Just One Kiss*, and one series, *Kings of the Castle* with New York Times and USA TODAY Bestselling authors. Her debut novel, *The Husband We Share*, hit the AALBC Bestsellers List within six months of release and was followed by her recent literary offerings: *Betrayal of Trust, King of Chatham, Sugarcoated Deception, and Deadly Deception*. She is a beta reader and a proud member of several writer's groups.

www.londonstcharles.com

FOLLOW LONDON ON SOCIAL MEDIA
Facebook: Author London St.Charles
Instagram: london_writes
Twitter:LSCharles2017

Chapter 1

"This is bigger than us. You of all people should understand that," Cadence said to Jackson while she folded her clothes and placed them inside a suitcase. She groaned something inaudible, walking the short distance from the oak chest of drawer and back to the bed, before lowering her body on the soft surface of the mattress.

"That's why?" Jackson said and rushed to her aid, sitting beside Cadence and propping his arm behind her for support. He placed his free hand on her protruding round belly, massaging it gently. "Are you in pain? Do I need to call your doctor?"

Cadence inhaled through her nostrils and exhaled slowly from her mouth in even intervals. Jackson removed the suitcase from the bed and lifted her legs, and placed a pillow underneath her head. He snatched his phone from his back pocket.

She gripped Jackson's wrist and squeezed, halting his movements, still breathing in the same fashion as before.

"Tell me what to do? What do you need me to do?"

After a few moments, she whispered, "Help me up."

The worried lines etched in Jackson's forehead never softened. "I need to get you to the hospital."

"I'm not in labor," Cadence assured him, holding her belly as she scooted to the edge of the bed. "Those were Braxton Hicks contractions."

"Braxton what?" he asked, glancing at her with skepticism.

"They mimic labor pains, but I promise you, that's all it was," she said, using Jackson's thigh for leverage, pushing herself into a standing position. "Could you pick the suitcase up from the floor?"

"This is absurd." Jackson fussed, closing the bedroom door. "You're seven months pregnant for Christ sakes. You don't need to be stuck on a plane for eleven hours. I bet Dr. Fischer wouldn't approve."

"He already did," Cadence countered, holding onto the bed and attempted to squat to lift the suitcase. "I wouldn't do anything to put our baby in danger."

"Just stop," Jackson warned, grabbing the luggage and placing it on the bed. "I can't believe he cleared you to fly."

"I'm only thirty-four weeks—— two weeks shy of the no-fly period," Cadence added, putting her lipstick and eyeliner in the travel makeup bag. "The trial shouldn't be any longer than one week, giving me enough time to get back and give birth to our baby boy."

Jackson folded his arms in protest.

"I wouldn't lie to you." She frowned, glaring at her husband. "You should know me better than that."

"It's not that, Cadence." Jackson ushered her to sit on the bench at the foot of the bed. "You make it all sound so simple. Seven months pregnant is seven months pregnant. Period. Sitting for long stretches already has an adverse effect on your body."

"I have to——"

"Plus," Jackson added, extending his index finger. "I'm not comfortable bringing Jackie back into that environment. Four years of therapy, learning that what Lester did to her wasn't her fault, along with getting accustomed to life without her mother." Jackson's breath hitched. "It's a lot. She's overcome so much, and being back in Chicago and facing Lester may be a trigger, causing a setback. It's not worth it, Cadence."

All of the reasons Jackson stated was exactly why Cadence needed to testify. Lester and Detective O'Brien had too much power over their lives, and it was time to put an end to their reign.

Four years ago, Cadence and her family moved to Stuttgart, the capital of the largest city of the German state of Braden-Württemberg. They needed a fresh start somewhere safe. The job offer from Cadence's employer, European automaker, Adali Automotive, couldn't have come at a better time, especially since she turned over evidence against Detective O'Brien that may put her family in danger.

"I'd understand if you didn't come with me," Cadence said with a hint of sadness.

"That's not an option," Jackson shot back. "Last time you insisted I stay behind——" Jackson's eyes watered. "That Detective O'Brien threatened—— and he ..."

Cadence winced, remembering that horrid incident when Detective O'Brien fondled her breasts with his service weapon and nonverbally threatened to rape her if she told anyone about his involvement with Lester or the circumstances surrounding Braelyn's death.

"Jackie could stay with my mother," she suggested as an alternative.

"Do you think that's a good idea?" Jackson asked, gazing at Cadence. "Phylicia has her own life."

"My mom adores Jackie, and you know it." Cadence gave Jackson a side-eye glance. "It's been over a year since the last time my mom's been here, and even longer for your parents."

Jackson's eyes bore into hers, and Cadence felt the depths of his pleading in her soul. "There's no way I can talk you out of this?"

"No," Cadence replied, squeezing Jackson's hand. "We've built a great life here in Stuttgart, but we should be able to travel back and forth to Chicago to visit our loved ones and not be afraid. I'm tired of living in the shadows. It's time that they were brought to justice."

"Testifying against Lester is one thing, but going against the Chicago Police Department is another," Jackson cautioned.

"Don't think for one second that this is going to go over without any hiccups."

"I'm praying that the recording I sent to the police headquarters and the fact that it's taken the department four years to investigate and bring them to trial is a good sign. I promise not to get too stressed out over this," she said, rubbing her tummy.

Jackson stooped, kissed Cadence's bulging belly-button, then pulled his packed suitcase from under the bed.

"What???" Cadence's mouth gaped open, nudging Jackson's head with her fingertips. "You made me go through all of that for nothing."

"I requested two weeks off over a month ago," Jackson countered, maneuvering the suitcase to the side. "The principal has a substitute Foreign Language English teacher in place. I wanted to give the school enough time to find someone." He paused, taking a seat beside Cadence. "Look, baby. Regardless if I like it or not, I'm going to support your decision either way. Though I was *really* hoping you would've changed your mind," Jackson admitted. "But remember … where you go, I go. That's never going to change."

Chapter 2

The following day, they arrived in Chicago and headed straight to Cadence's mother's house. The wintry weather in January was warmer than they were used to in Stuttgart.

Phylicia opened the door of her three-bedroom raised-ranch home in the Morgan Park neighborhood and swooped her daughter in her arms. Tears soaked Phylicia's shoulder as Cadence cried from the overwhelming happiness in her heart.

"Mama, I've missed you so much," Cadence mumbled, wiping her tear-stained face.

"I'm so glad I get to hold you in my arms," Phylicia replied. "FaceTime just isn't enough," she said, smiling and touching Cadence's belly. Phylicia looked around until her eyes landed on Jackie. "I bet you're going to be an amazing big sister." She winked and extended her arms.

"Hi, grandma." Jackie pressed her body into Phylicia's and held on tight.

"Save some of them hugs for me," Jackson teased and embraced Phylicia, smashing Jackie in the middle like an Oreo sandwich cookie.

Cadence laughed as Jackie's muffled voice whispered, "Grandma, you're smooshing me."

"I have a little surprise for you guys——"

"Mom, you didn't have to do anything," Cadence whined as Jackson helped her out of her coat.

"I know there's a seven-hour time difference between here and Germany, and you're all jet-lagged, but trust me," Phylicia said with a twinkle in her eye, "Y'all are going to love it."

Jackson glanced at Cadence, then at Jackie. "I wonder what your granny has up her sleeve."

They walked into the living room, decorated in rust brown and copper, through the formal dining room with the crystal chandelier hanging low over the table set for six, then into the large kitchen.

"Is that peach cobbler I smell?" Cadence sniffed, leaning onto the counter for support.

"Smells just like my mom's," Jackson chimed in and kissed his mother-in-law on the cheek. "No disrespect to the cook."

"None taken," an elderly woman's voice said from behind them.

"Grandma Ella," Jackie screamed, wrapping her arms around the silver-haired woman.

Jackson cupped Ella's face in his hands. "Momma," he cried, embracing the first woman he'd ever loved. "It's so good to see you. Where's dad?"

"I'm coming," Thomas blurted out, rounding the corner from the guest bedroom. "This old man isn't as fast as he used to be. Your momma done wore me down." He chuckled.

"Your father has always been a cut-up," Ella commented, shaking her head.

"Now, I'm a cut-down, trying to keep up with that foxy lady."

Laughter erupted, filling the house with a wholesome feeling that Cadence had been missing since the move.

Lester and Detective O'Brien had to be found guilty. Cadence needed to be in the presence of her family more often, and her children needed to feel the love of their grandparents.

"Darling, don't cry," Phylicia said, handing Cadence a paper towel.

"All of us haven't been under the same roof in years. Maybe it's the hormones—— I don't know," Cadence replied, dabbing her eyes. "My kids need to know what it feels like to be spoiled by their grandparents on the regular. Not only when you guys can come to visit. They need to be loved, hugged, and fussed over the way I was when I visited granny and pops."

"Soon," Ella said, placing a weathered hand on Cadence's back and glanced at Phylicia. "Real soon."

* * *

A few hours later, Cadence and her family arrived home. She released a delightful sigh, smiling at the light burning in the concrete snow lantern along the stone path of the Japanese garden. Cadence stepped inside, and fresh lemon and pine infused her nostrils. She grazed her hand along the back of the sofa, and not a speck of dust rested in the crease of her fingers. The maid she hired took great care of her home, even stocking the fridge before their arrival.

Jackie was supposed to stay overnight at her grandma Phylicia's house, but she was eager to come home, and Cadence couldn't deny her that. They'd take Jackie in the morning before heading to court.

After dinner, Jackie laid on the queen-sized bed with her laptop in the guest bedroom on the main floor across the hall from her parents' room.

"Why are you sleeping down here?" Cadence asked since Jackie's room was upstairs. "It's not a problem. I was just curious."

"No reason really." Jackie shrugged, her attention still focused on the laptop screen. "I didn't feel like being up there tonight."

"That's fine, but don't stay up too late," Cadence warned, shuffling into the master bedroom with Jackson walking close behind with his hands resting on her hips.

"I'm not sleepy," Jackie replied, twirling her ankles. "It's only nine-thirty."

"But it's four-thirty in the morning in Germany," Cadence shouted over her shoulder, walking in her room and slowly climbing into bed. "I don't know how she does it. I'm ready to pass out."

"Let me worry about Jackie for the evening," Jackson said in a soft tone while placing a pillow underneath Cadence's legs. "All you need to do is relax. I got you," he teased, massaging her swollen feet while gazing at her with hooded bedroom eyes.

"Don't start something you can't finish," she moaned, closing her eyes. "You know that's how this baby got here."

"Yeah, I know," Jackson agreed as he circled and applied soothing pressure to the bottom of her feet. "That means I get to play; however, I choose since there aren't any consequences."

"Well come on then," she slurred, already half asleep.

Jackson climbed alongside Cadence and kissed her lips and then her belly. "Goodnight," he whispered, pulling the quilt over Cadence and leaving the bed.

"Where—— are you—— going?"

"To get our things set for the morning." He laughed. "Sleep tight."

"Don't let the bed bugs bite," Jackie shouted from her bedroom.

* * *

Cadence pulled the covers over her face at the sudden flickering light that filtered through the room. She lifted her arms above her head, yawned, extended her legs, and was careful not to point her toes so she wouldn't get a Charlie horse. Never opening her eyes, she rolled on her side, turning her back toward the disturbance that had interrupted her sleep. Cadence snuggled the pillow and tried to get comfortable, but sleep wouldn't revisit her anytime soon. She yanked the quilt away from her face, opened her eyes, and they collided with blue lights dancing on the wall.

"What?" she moaned, turning over and seeing bright police lights coming through the bedroom window. "Jackson," she called out, sliding on a pair of slippers.

Cadence swung open the bedroom door and almost tripped over Jackie.

"Why are you sitting in the doorway?" Cadence asked, holding onto the wooden frame.

"Daddy told me to."

"Get up from there." Cadence, frowned. "What's going on?"

"Mama Cee, I'm scared." Jackie laid her head on Cadence's belly. "Someone tried to break-in the house."

"Go into the bedroom and close the door. Don't come out until I tell you," Cadence instructed, sliding past Jackie.

"But daddy said——"

"Don't worry about daddy."

Scattered glass and stones from the contemporary Japanese landscaped front yard, covered the hardwood living room floor. Cadence treaded around the jagged objects carefully, then stepped outside into the frigid night air without a coat.

Four squad cars were parked in front of their house. Her

eyes zeroed in on the garden—— or what was left of it. She paid someone year-round to maintain it, even while they were in Germany. The concrete snow lantern was cracked, the bamboo bridge was egged, the stone path made up of rare stones imported from Japan were streaked in yellow paint, and the words, 'You a dead bitch' was spray-painted across the frozen grass.

Heat rushed through her body, and it wasn't from pregnancy hormones. Cadence headed down the stairs, but Jackson cut her off. "Baby, you need to go back inside. I've already talked to the——"

"What happened?"

"I was in the basement ironing when I heard glass breaking. The alarm sounded, and Jackie screamed. I ran upstairs to check on you all when a ton of rocks flew through the window. One hit me," Jackson explained, rubbing the back of his head. "I thought I'd been shot. I looked in on you and called them," he said, pointing toward the officers. "I don't know how you slept through that."

"We haven't been here twelve hours, and the bullshit has already started," Cadence growled through clenched teeth. "They don't scare me, Jackson. I *will* be in court tomorrow."

"I know, baby." He nodded, clasping her shoulders. "Please. Please. Please, go back inside."

Cadence glared at the cops who were dusting for fingerprints and taking pictures. "For all I know, one of them probably did this."

Chapter 3

Jackson didn't want to feed into Cadence's line of thinking, but she was probably right. He was fuming on the inside because deep down, he knew something was going to happen; he just didn't expect it to be the first night they came back.

He swept up the glass and rocks while the board-up company secured the living room windows. Then Jackson went into the basement and found a couple of old cans of green spray paint and covered the derogatory words across the lawn, but not before taking pictures of his own for evidence.

"Daddy, I'm scared," Jackie cried as she leaped into his arms, almost knocking him over. "I wanna go home."

Jackson's lungs filled to the point his chest burned. He held Jackie tight against his body and stroked her thick curls.

He lowered onto the loveseat, catching a glimpse of Cadence backed into the corner with her hands covering her mouth and nose.

"Releasing his breath," Jackson replied, "This is your other home. Where all of our family lives."

"I don't like it here. Nothing like this ever happened in Stuttgart," Jackie said, wiping the tears from her eyes with the back of her hand. "Why did we have to come here?"

He purposely avoided eye contact with Cadence. Jackson felt the same as his baby girl, but he understood why they had to do it. Cadence needed justice as well as closure, and he didn't want to make her feel bad for doing what was necessary.

"We are visiting grandma and ..."

Cadence shuffled over, caressed Jackie's face, and peered at Jackson while shaking her head. She didn't have to utter a word. Jackson understood the look. They were connected that way.

He scooted over, giving Cadence enough room to sit beside him.

"We promised always to tell each other the truth, right?" he said to Jackie.

"Yeah," she responded just above a whisper.

"You might not remember because this happened a long time ago," Jackson explained, pushing Jackie's hair from her face. "Do you remember the policeman who asked Cadence to get in his car the night your mommy died?"

Jackie's eyes narrowed, and her lips twisted.

It took every ounce of self-control for Jackson not to show

any emotion. He hated bringing this up, especially after they worked so hard to get past the tragedy.

"Sort of—— I mean, I remember parts of it."

"That policeman did a bad thing, and I have to go to court to tell the judge what I know," Cadence explained, rubbing Jackson's hand that rested along Jackie's back.

"I thought the police were supposed to protect us."

"They are," Jackson said. "But all of them aren't good people. Most of them are, and if you're ever in trouble, you should call 911, but sometimes there's one or two that don't do the right thing."

"Kind of like the kids in your classroom," Cadence added. "Most of them do their work and listen to the teacher, but there's always one or two that get in trouble."

"Yeah, like Jonas and Fynn." Jackie chuckled, sitting upright on her father's lap. "They always give Ms. Schneider a hard time. She starts yelling, and she always ends up sending them to the office."

"Exactly," Cadence said, shifting on the loveseat. "Me testifying in court is like sending the policeman to the office. The judge is the principal."

Jackson loved how Cadence had a way of relating to Jackie. She talked to her like the ten-year-old she was while being honest in a way that she understood.

"Give me big hugs," Jackson said, wrapping his arms around Jackie and squeezing her tight. "You too, mommy." He smiled at Cadence and put his arms around her.

"We love you," Cadence cooed, kissing Jackie on the

forehead.

"I love you more," Jackie responded, squealing as Jackson picked her up and carried her over his shoulder to the bedroom. He placed Jackie in the bed and tucked her underneath the turquoise comforter with ruffles. "Have a goodnight, sweetheart. I love you."

"Goodnight, daddy."

Jackson blew her a kiss, turned off the light, and pulled the door closed.

Before going back into the living room with Cadence, he made a phone call.

"Hey, Sly."

"Yooooo, Jax. My dude," Sly yelled into the phone, causing Jackson's eardrum to throb. "Whaddup, cousin?"

"Sly——"

"How's Germany treating you, and when are you bringing your ass home?" he asked in that loud hospitable tone.

"I'm back in Chicago," Jackson countered, stepping into the bathroom and closing the door. He turned the water on in the sink before he continued. "I need——"

"Guess who's back in the Chi, Tony?" he shouted to his twin brother. "Just wait till Aunt Mable finds out. She's been———"

"Hey, man. Hey. Hold up a minute," Jackson shouted over Sly, then lowered his voice. "I need you to listen."

"You got the floor, l'il cousin."

"Do you remember what I wrote about, explaining the reason we left?"

"Yeah. That punk ass cop and Lester threatened Cadence. Is he still bothering y'all? Where you at? You need me to roll through?"

"We had an incident here at the house, but we're good," Jackson said, listening for Cadence's footsteps.

"What the fuck happened?" Sly questioned, his tone aggressive and hostile. "Yo, Tony. We gotta make a run."

"Slow down, Sly."

Jackson knew the twin duo would handle their business. They were street-savvy and had a rep to back it up. Over the years, they smoothed out their street persona, and to the layman person, Sly and Tony were regular men who dressed in slacks, button-downs, carried a briefcase, and went to their respective jobs. But to the folks in the hood, they were known as thugs in a suit who protected their community. No one ever crossed them and lived to tell about it.

They loved them some Cadence, and she returned their affections, but she'd have Jackson's ass if she saw them lurking outside of their home. The twins were trouble, but Jackson loved his cousins, and they needed their help. He didn't trust these crooked cops to do their job.

"I need eyes and ears on the streets, my parents' house, Cadence's mom's, and at the crib ... *discreetly*," Jackson warned. "Cadence can't know anything about this."

"Consider it handled."

Chapter 4

They arrived an hour early at the Cook County Criminal Court Building. Protestors of all races swarmed the sidewalk and street with picket signs causing a major traffic jam. Tensions ran high in Chicago, after the sentencing of a former police officer, Jason Van Dyke. He received less than seven years in prison for murdering the black seventeen-year-old, Laquan McDonald. This was an injustice to the human race, but specifically for African Americans.

Cadence followed the case while in Germany and understood the public's outrage. The outcome made her leery of her case against Detective O'Brien. There was irrefutable proof of Van Dyke's guilt. The whole world saw the video, and he still got a slap on the wrist. All Cadence had was an audio recording of Detective O'Brien's voice. What were the odds of her receiving justice?

Jackson gripped Cadence's hand and led her through the frustrating protestors. Once they entered the building, Cadence and Jackson had to go through security, placing their items in a plastic bin, then onto a conveyor belt.

The alarm attached above the metal detector sounded as Cadence walked through the body scanner.

"What the fu …" she mumbled under her breath. She didn't have anything in her pockets to warrant the alarm.

"Please step over here," said the man in dark brown pants and a tan shirt with a Cook County Sheriff's badge on his sleeve.

Cadence did as she was instructed while glancing backward at Jackson as he came through the metal detector without any issues. Jackson collected his watch and belt, along with Cadence's belongings, then stood to the side to wait for her.

"Arms out," the sheriff commanded, holding a black wand in his hand.

He traced the outline of Cadence's body; no detection of metal was found. Then he waved the wand in front of her breast, and Cadence flinched, but still, no trace of metal was present.

She trembled, instantly flashing back to Detective O'Brien, sliding his service weapon between her breast to intimidate and ensure her silence of his involvement with Lester.

The sheriff eyed Cadence longer than she deemed necessary, making her more uncomfortable than she already was.

"What's the hold-up?" Jackson asked, inching forward.

The sheriff frowned, placing a hand over the holster on his waist. He never acknowledged Jackson nor averted his glare from Cadence. "System glitch." He shrugged. "You're free to go."

Cadence placed a protective hand over her belly as she walked toward Jackson and whispered, "Are these *coincidences and glitches* going to happen for the duration of the trial?"

Jackson cast an evil glare at the sheriff. "I think we need to be prepared for the unexpected," he said, holding her hand as they proceeded to the elevators.

* * *

The courtroom was evenly divided. The boys in blue flooded the left-hand side, and the undesirables, dressed in sagging jeans, oversized white t-shirts, and snapback caps, on the right.

Cadence stood as tall as her pregnant belly would allow as both group's eyes bore through her as she slid into the back row of the gallery. She'd be lying if she said the attention wasn't unsettling.

"Are you alright, baby?" Jackson asked, grabbing her coat and folding it over his arm, then placing a hand on her thigh. "You're shaking."

"No, I'm not," she shot back, glancing down at her arms and hands.

"Your insides," Jackson whispered in her ear. "I feel you," he said, lightly squeezing her thigh.

"I can't wait until this is over with, so we can get back to our life before Detective O'Brien and Lester ever entered our existence," she said, peering beyond the spectators, landing her focus on the cocky detective with his attorney in the front of the courtroom. "He's finally going to get what he deserves."

"All rise," the bailiff instructed, "Honorable Judge Clark Duncan presiding."

The raven-haired judge dawning a black robe with a white shirt and red tie peeking from the collar, stepped up to the elevated platform and took a seat behind the bench, where he had the power to change people's lives with the bang of a gavel. He looked out to the gallery and said, "You may be seated."

Other than the movement from people lowering onto their bottoms, not a single word was spoken.

"I know emotions are running high at this time with several cases pending against the Chicago Police Department, but at no time will any outburst be allowed in *my* courtroom," Judge Duncan said in a tone that meant business. "If you can't conduct yourself in an orderly fashion, this would be the time to excuse yourself."

Cadence nodded, taking a deep breath as the judge looked out into the gallery. Jackson interlocked his fingers with hers, and that settled her nerves a bit.

"Very well. Let's get started." Judge Duncan put on a

pair of silver, wired glasses, then slid them to the tip of his nose while looking down at the document before him. "The people versus Paul O'Brien with conspiracy charges to cover up a crime and witness intimidation. The defendant entered a plea of 'not guilty' at the preliminary hearing," the judge said, removing the frames and leaning back in his seat. "Prosecution, your opening statement."

Assistant District Attorney, Aaron Knox, stood, fastening the button on his grey suit jacket. "Your Honor, may I approach the bench?"

Cadence tilted her head and whispered, "That can't be good."

"What do you mean?" Jackson asked, glancing at Cadence, then the front of the courtroom as both attorneys walked toward the bench.

"The trial hasn't even started, and there's a problem." Cadence frowned as Judge Duncan placed a hand over the microphone. "I wonder what's wrong."

Judge Duncan pursed his thick lips. His trimmed brows knotted, and his eyes narrowed.

"I knew it," she said, leaning forward.

The Judge said something that resulted in a satisfying smirk across Detective O'Brien's attorney's face as he maneuvered back to the defendant's counsel table. Cadence bit her lip and shook her head. ADA Knox didn't appear half as confident as he walked back to the prosecution table. She swore his forehead was glistening from beads of sweat.

"Your Honor," Detective O'Brien's attorney said, his arms

moved like a ballroom dancer with every word he spoke. "In light of this new information, I ask that all charges against my client be dropped."

Gasps and whispers from the gallery filled the courtroom. Cadence's unborn son must have sensed the uprising as he kicked her ribcage with such force that she lunged forward and cried out. Immediately, her hands drew to the source of the pain.

Jackson wrapped his arms around her. "Let's get out of here," he said, rubbing her back. "This isn't good for you or the baby."

"I'm not going anywhere until I find out what's going on," Cadence countered, massaging the area below her left breast.

The pounding gavel grabbed everyone's attention.

"Order in the court. Order in the court," Judge Duncan demanded, wearing an exasperated expression. "Mr. Reed, don't get ahead of yourself."

"The prosecution has the burden of proof, Your Honor," Reed commented, gesturing toward ADA Knox. "And the only evidence—— alleged evidence linking my client to any crime, has been compromised."

Cadence grabbed Jackson's arm, digging her nails into his skin to keep from speaking what was on the tip of her tongue. Incompetence. Railroaded. Cover-up. Injustice were just a few of the words that came to mind.

"Your Honor," ADA Knox pleaded, "The people request a sixty-day continuance to restructure our case."

"The prosecution has had more than enough time to gather

evidence," Reed interjected.

"He has a point," Judge Duncan replied. "The time to ask for a continuance is before the trial starts, Mr. Knox."

"Your Honor, I left the office at approximately eleven o'clock last night," Knox explained. "I wasn't aware that the office had been vandalized until seven a.m. when I went to retrieve the files and evidence for trial. There was no way for me to inform the court until now."

"Seems like the ADA needs to beef up their security," Reed said, glancing at Knox with that same smirk on his face.

Detective O'Brien sat stoically, unfazed by it all, and that enraged Cadence. The slow simmer that burned inside of her was threatening to burst at any moment. Her nails dug deeper into Jackson's skin.

"That's enough," Judge Duncan warned Reed, angling a steely gaze at him. Then, he turned his attention to Mr. Knox. "You have thirty days."

Judge Duncan banged the gavel, and Cadence flinched, relaxing the grip on Jackson, but only a tad.

"Vandalized. Thirty days," Cadence whispered, glancing at her husband as he lifted her fingers one-by-one from his arm, then closed his hands around hers. "That's right before the baby is due," Cadence said, staring at the deep red marks embedded in Jackson's skin.

"We'll figure it out," Jackson soothed, massaging her fingers. "I'll call the job and extend my leave."

"Excuse me, Mr. and Mrs. Goldsmith," ADA Knox interrupted, standing over them from the aisle.

Cadence's head jerked upward. The man before her didn't exude power and lacked confidence. "You've got some explaining to do."

Chapter 5

"I take it we can't go to your office and have this conversation," Cadence said to ADA Knox, not masking the disappointment in her voice.

He parted his lips to respond but held his tongue as the last of the spectators and officers left the courtroom. Cadence did a double-take as one of the men's side profile looked familiar.

"Crime scene investigators have taken over my office and the entire ninth floor for the foreseeable future," Knox replied, unbuttoning his suit jacket, then taking a seat in the row directly in front of them. He placed the leather briefcase next to him, then threw his arm across the back of the bench, angling his body toward Jackson and Cadence. "We're going to get them. Don't worry."

"All she can do is worry," Jackson shot back, agitation evident in his tone. "You told my wife that this would be over in a week. Now, another thirty days has been tacked onto this farce."

"What happened this morning?" Cadence asked, folding her hands atop her belly.

"I went to collect my things for court, and the door to my office was ajar," he explained, loosening his maroon necktie. "The door didn't appear to be tampered with or damaged in any way, and I *know* I locked it before I left last night; there isn't any doubt in my mind."

Cadence glanced around the courtroom to make sure they were still alone. "So, you're saying this was an inside job."

"Looks that way," Knox agreed. "Whoever it was, had a key."

"Playing devil's advocate here," Jackson said with a slight shrug. "Maybe the custodian forgot to lock up."

One of the things Cadence loved most about her husband was that he always gave people the benefit of the doubt. This time he was so far off the mark. Cadence believed he knew it when he asked the question.

"No one has access to my office unless I'm present, and the door stays locked at all times due to the nature of the files that I store. Even if that was the case, how would you explain the flash drive, Cadence's phone, and all the files pertaining to only *this* case missing?" Knox questioned, his eggshell skin flushed scarlet. "Someone turned over the desk, cracking the computer screen, and broke into six of the eight secured file cabinets."

"That's no coincidence," she remarked, glancing over at Jackson. "Our home was vandalized last night, too."

Knox's eyes grew wider by the second. "Did you report it?"

"I did," Jackson cut in, leaning forward. "I'm not going to put up with my family's life being threatened," he warned in a tone that made every hair on Cadence's body bristle.

"*You a dead bitch* was spray-painted across the grass," Cadence added, staring at Knox. "They really don't want me to testify."

Knox shook his head.

"This isn't the first grievance against Detective O'Brien. Every complaint against him has been thrown out because the victims are too afraid to come forward," he admitted, tapping his finger on the back of the bench. "I've suspected witness intimidation for a long time, but no one would ever confirm it. The victims either say, they've changed their mind, or they don't remember what happened," Knox said, pointing his index finger at Cadence. "But you're the first one to follow through, *and* you got him on tape. The department is running scared. What other reason would there be for the events that took place at your home and my office?"

Cadence let that hang in the air.

"So, there are others?" she queried, shifting in her seat to relieve the pressure the baby was putting on her tailbone.

"Yes." Knox hesitated for a moment. "And I've gotten two of the women to agree to testify as long as they knew the recording would be played and it wouldn't be just their word against his. And …"

Cadence shot a glance at Jackson, then back to Knox.

"What aren't you telling us?" Jackson asked the question that was on the tip of Cadence's tongue.

Knox gave a half-smile. "The other deciding factor was that *you* testified."

"Why didn't you tell me that?" Cadence said in a raised voice, but not loud enough for the sheriffs to come rushing the courtroom.

"Because I didn't want to put any added pressure on you," Knox revealed with a sheepish expression.

"This is a big deal," Jackson admonished. "You can't keep pertinent information from us."

Knox nodded at Jackson, then Cadence. "It won't happen again."

"I'm glad we understand each other," Jackson responded.

"Thank you," Cadence said, fidgeting her wedding band that hung on a gold rope around her neck due to her fingers swelling.

Knox scanned the area, then leaned further over the back of the bench. Cadence and Jackson scooted forward, closing the gap between them.

"I've also learned that Detective O'Brien's on the south eastside gang and drug lord's payroll——"

"You mean, Lester?" Cadence crossed her arms over her

larger than normal breasts.

"I'll never forgive him for what he did to Jackie and Braelyn." Jackson frowned, causing his handsome features to obscure. "It took years of therapy to help Jackie through the havoc Lester brought into her life. No child should have to endure the murder of her mother and molestation from the same monster."

Now, it was Cadence's turn to comfort him. She stroked the back of Jackson's head and neck.

She witnessed firsthand the trauma that Jackie had experienced. Back then, she never wanted to be a mom, but Jackie was the blessing Cadence didn't know she needed. Cadence embraced Jackson's daughter with open arms and has loved Jackie as her own ever since.

"Has Lester been located?" she asked, focusing on Jackson, but directing the question to Knox.

"Not yet," Knox replied, placing a hand on Cadence's shoulder. "But you don't have to worry about the evidence against him. We have his prints from the gun that was found at the crime scene already in the system. That same gun has five bodies on it," Knox revealed. "We also have a BOLO for Lester in the states surrounding Illinois. If he sets foot anywhere in the Midwest, he's going down."

That gave Cadence some comfort, but not much. It had been four years. Lester may already be in Chicago somewhere, laying low. She would keep her thoughts to herself. The last thing she wanted to do was worry Jackson.

"I'm not sure how to proceed since the recording's

missing?" Knox admitted, pinching the bridge of his nose. "That's why I asked for sixty days. I knew Judge Duncan wouldn't grant that much time. Over the years, I've learned to ask for more than what I need, and he'll order somewhere in the ballpark of what I actually want."

Cadence grabbed the bench in front of her and released a labored sigh.

"Baby, are you alright?" Jackson asked, placing a hand under her elbow.

"Just a little uncomfortable," she replied, scooting to the edge of the seat and resting her head against the wood. "I'm ready to go. Are we done?"

"Yes." Knox stood, grabbing the briefcase. "I'll be in touch," he said, extending a hand to Jackson. "Take care of her."

"Always."

Cadence raised a hand, acknowledging the sentiment as she willed the continuous pain on her tailbone to subside.

Once Knox left the courtroom, and the chatter in the hallway faded, Cadence let out a cry.

"Is it your tailbone?"

She closed her eyes tight and nodded.

"Come on, baby." Jackson helped Cadence to her feet, massaging her backside with the base of the palm of his hand as she leaned over the bench.

After ten minutes, the pain had vanished. Cadence couldn't have been more grateful for her husband than at that moment. Jackson always knew how to take care of her, and what he didn't know; he was willing to learn.

He lifted her coat, and Cadence slid her arms inside the sleeves. Jackson pushed open the oversized, heavy oak door, and held it until Cadence passed through into the hallway. They took only a few steps when a man in a tan suit with blonde hair and the same translucent-blue eyes as Jackie's, bounded from a bench, landing in front of them.

"Steven Bekker." Cadence flinched at the sight of her work nemesis from Adali Automotive's Chicago office, who also happened to be Jackie's uncle. "I thought that was you. What are you doing here?"

Chapter 6

Cadence hadn't given Steven much thought since her promotion four years ago. He'd finally gotten what he always coveted, her title as Chief Design Officer. It only took her accepting the full-time position with a higher pay grade to run the parent company in Stuttgart, Germany, for it to happen.

She glanced at Jackson before asking Steven, who seemed to be in a trance, a second time, "What are you doing here?"

"Um—— hey—— sorry for staring," he said, sliding hands into his pockets. "I didn't know you were expecting." Steven crossed his arms as the corner of his lip twitched. "They must be treating you *really* good over there in Germany if you had time to get knocked up and still run the Global company. Congratulations—— to both of you."

That's the Steven she remembered. He always had a snide remark when it came to her. Cadence gave him a quick scan. His once shiny blonde hair appeared dull, and he had put on more than a few pounds. Steven didn't have a six-pound baby inside of him and edema to justify his weight gain. What excuse did he have for letting himself go? She could reply to his off-brand remark with that, but why bother.

"What do you want?" Jackson asked; his tone was rigid and accompanied by a baffled expression.

Cadence knew Jackson still blamed Steven for the role he played in bringing Braelyn and Lester into their lives. Even though it was messy, they would have never found out about Jackie if the circumstances hadn't unfolded the way they did.

She had her own reasons for not wanting to be bothered with Steven. Cadence dropped him in the bucket with the other people who meant her no good. She'd forgiven his actions a long time ago, but she would never forget them.

"I had a feeling you would be here today," he said, putting his focus on Cadence. "I've been wanting——" Steven mumbled, lowering his gaze to the floor. He inhaled sharply, then lifted his eyes until they were boring into hers. "Can we go somewhere and talk?"

"About what?" she asked, leaning on Jackson, taking some of the pressure off of her aching feet. "Never mind. I don't want to know."

"I want to meet Jackie," he blurted out.

"No. Why?" Jackson fired back before Cadence could say anything. "My baby doesn't need you in her life."

"I would like to get to know my niece."

"Why now?" Cadence asked.

"I always had, but with everything that was going on——and then you all disappeared off the grid," Steven said in a softer tone that sounded genuine. "I never had the chance to say anything … until now."

Cadence stared at him for a long time. There could be some truth in his statement, but it was Steven, and it was hard to accept anything he said at face value.

"Why should I trust you?" she asked.

"I know I've never given you much reason to in the past," Steven admitted, reaching into the inner pocket of his suit jacket, pulled out a pen, and a business card, then scribbled something on the back of it. "But I'm not the same man you remember."

Cadence glanced at the security guard who stood at his post with his hands folded at his waist a few feet away.

"You don't have to make a decision today, but please think about it and give me a call when you're ready," Steven said, placing the card in her hand. "I hope to hear from you soon."

* * *

"What do you think?" Cadence asked Jackson as he pulled out of the parking lot on their way to pick Jackie up from her mother's house.

"I don't like it." He huffed, making a sharp turn onto Twenty-Sixth Street. "And I don't appreciate him ambushing us at the courthouse."

Cadence stared out of the window toward the people at the bus stop. "Is it something you'd consider?"

"Do you think I should?"

"I don't know." She shrugged, observing a woman pulling a Spiderman skullcap down over a young boy's ears. "Steven seemed sincere, and ... he is her uncle. It'd be nice for Jackie to connect with him as long as he's on the level," Cadence said, touching Jackson's thigh. "But you have to do what you feel is right."

Jackson was quiet for several minutes, leaving Cadence wondering what he was thinking.

"Maybe Jackie would have a chance to meet her maternal grandmother, Irene. She could tell her stories about her mom as a young girl," Cadence said, leaning against the headrest, facing Jackson. "I'm sure Jackie would love that."

"She would." Jackson smiled and shot a quick glance at Cadence as he drove underneath the rusted viaduct, approaching the intersection of Twenty-Sixth Street and Western Avenue. "Thanks for being my voice of reason. I'll give Steven a call after——"

"Watch out," Cadence screamed at the sight of an eighteen-wheeler barreling down the wrong side of the street, heading straight for them.

She clutched her stomach as Jackson swerved to the far-right lane, scraping the concrete wall. Orange sparks flew from the side of the car like fireworks on New Year's Eve. Jackson unbuckled his seatbelt and threw his body on top of Cadence.

"Hold on, baby," he shouted just as the truck crushed the driver's side like a compactor at the junkyard.

Chapter 7

"Shit," Jackson roared, clutching Cadence as glass and metal objects flew everywhere. He gritted his teeth from the sharp pain radiating in his lower calf. For a split second, Jackson thought his right leg had been severed, but then, his ankle twitched.

"Are you okay?" he asked, raising his head only to get violently jerked forward, causing his front teeth to slam into Cadence's forehead.

"Ooooouch," she cried, holding onto his sides.

Jackson tried to shake off the throbbing pain that took

over his entire face from the impact just as the car got snatched again in a vicious game of tug of war. He held onto Cadence's headrest and peered over her head as the eighteen-wheeler detached itself from their vehicle, dragging the rear bumper down the street as a souvenir.

The full-sized vehicle had been reduced to a single-row bobsled.

"Are you hurt?" he asked, attempting to lift his body off of hers. Jackson was sure his full weight on top of Cadence wasn't good for the baby. He'd be lost if anything happened to either one of them.

"My insides are doing something funky," she groaned. "Like every nerve ending in my body is jumping, and I feel dampness between my legs."

Dear God, please let my son be okay.

"Are you folks alright," a masculine voice shouted, but Jackson couldn't see anyone from his position.

"My wife's pregnant," Jackson shouted, still trying to alleviate some of the pressure he was putting on Cadence's belly.

"Help's on the way," the man said, maneuvering to the side of the vehicle. He tried to pry what was left of the mangled door open, but it wouldn't budge. "Hey, man. What's your name?"

"Jackson," he replied, glancing down at her. "I think she's bleeding."

"I'm Floyd. I'm going to stay right here until help arrives."

"Cadence baby, you hear that," Jackson wiggled her

shoulder, but she didn't respond. "Wake up, Cadence," he said, shaking her harder. "Stay with me, baby."

"My husband owns a tow truck company around the corner," a tall woman said, standing next to Floyd, breathless. "He's on his way with the hitch so we can get y'all out of there."

"You're not supposed to move them," another male voice said, but Jackson didn't see anyone near Floyd or the other woman. He must've been standing in front of the car. "You can cause more damage. Wait for the paramedics."

Cadence lifted her head, and Jackson let out a sigh of relief.

"Baby, you scared me," he smothered her face with kisses. "Try to stay awake."

"That's—— that's——" She lifted her arm, pointing straight ahead, then her eyes closed and head slumped.

"Cadence!!!!"

* * *

"Where am I?"

Jackson raised his head from the bed and pushed back his chair. He leaned forward and stroked Cadence's hair. "The hospital."

"Why?" she asked, maneuvering her hand toward her belly, but Jackson grabbed it and kissed her fingers. Reaching for the chair with his good leg, he pulled it close enough to lower into the seat, never letting her hand go.

"We were in a car accident."

"No wonder I feel like I've been run over by a semi," she

winced, sliding her free hand to her midsection. "My lower abdomen is killing me, especially on the left side."

Jackson didn't know what to say. She hadn't mentioned the baby. Did Cadence even remember she was pregnant?

"I need to tell you something."

"What is it?" she asked, pushing the controls on the side rail, adjusting the tilt of the bed.

Jackson smiled and perched on the edge of the mattress. "We are the parents of a beautiful, *healthy*, baby boy."

Cadence eyes narrowed as her hands slid in slow motion across her stomach. Her mouth opened and her eyes grew to the size of golf balls.

"It's too soon," she wailed, digging her heels into the mattress. "That truck hit us. Ooooh …"

"Everything's okay," Jackson comforted, rubbing her thigh. "You had an emergency c-section."

She shook her head, and tears welled in her lower eyelids.

"Our son is a survivor. *You,* my love, are a survivor." Jackson smiled, thanking the man above for covering his family.

Cadence had fluid in her belly, which added pressure on the baby, making it hard for him to receive oxygen. They had to deliver him to save both of their lives.

"Where is he?" Cadence asked, scanning the room.

"Caden Jackson Goldsmith is in the NICU," the woman in pink scrubs said, pumping the hand sanitizer dispenser as she entered the room. "I'm Dr. Garrison."

Cadence stroked her husband's cheek. "Caden … you

named him after me?"

"You said I could make him a junior." Jackson tilted his head and winked. "So, I did."

The tears finally trickled from Cadence's eyes. Jackson leaned over, placing his lips softly against hers. "I love you. Don't you know there's nothing I won't do for you?"

"I'm Dr. Garrison," she said, blinking several times. "We're not about to do this again. Your husband had the entire delivery team in tears. This man loves you."

"Yes, he does." Cadence grinned, adjusting on the bed. "Hi, Dr. Garrison. When can I see my baby?"

"Soon, I promise, but I need you to be careful of your movements. I don't want you to tear your stitches."

"I'll make sure she takes it easy," Jackson added. "Can you explain to her what you told me?"

Dr. Garrison gave a warm smile. It eased Jackson's nerves, and he prayed it did the same for Cadence.

"Caden is thirty-four weeks, weighing four and a half pounds and nineteen inches long. He's considered a moderately preterm baby, which means he will not spend much time in the NICU, and his complications should be few," she explained, stepping closer to the bed. "That being said, we still need to keep a close eye on him."

Jackson rolled his hand over Cadence's.

"His immune health is compromised since the respiratory system doesn't fully develop until the last weeks of pregnancy. He'll need help breathing for a short time, but that's expected. Caden's biggest challenge will be learning to eat."

"Why is that?" Jackson asked. "I thought it was natural for babies to suckle."

"It is, once he's full term, but Caden's suck-swallow-breath reflex isn't developed enough yet, and it'll make it hard for him to take in enough nourishment to grow and gain weight."

"So, what do I need to do?" Cadence inquired, gazing at the doctor.

"Love him. Visit him as much as possible," Dr. Garrison replied, holding onto the bedrail. "Talk to him. The sound of your voice will be soothing and familiar. Let Caden know he's not alone. Preterm babies who are visited often by their parents fair so much better than those who aren't."

"Thank you so much," Jackson said, standing.

"You're quite welcome. I'll have a nurse take you to the NICU," Dr. Garrison said while checking Cadence's vitals and incision. "Fair warning, you won't be able to hold him just yet, neither of you are ready for that," she explained, removing the thermometer from Cadence's mouth. "And don't be alarmed by the tubes, wiring, and beeping sounds. Though they can be a bit overwhelming, keep in mind that they are necessary for the baby's health."

"Thanks again." Jackson raised his hand toward heaven. "What a mighty God we serve."

"I agree," Dr. Garrison said, pointing down at Jackson's ripped, bloodstained pant leg. "Now, go get yourself checked out."

Chapter 8

"Whatever they bring me is gonna taste like steak and potatoes," Cadence said to Jackson, rubbing her hands together, checking the time on the wall clock across the room.

The doctor finally gave the okay for her to eat solid foods.

"Woman, it's only been three days."

"I'd like to see you go just one day on a liquid diet, then talk to me."

Jackson splayed his hands in the air. "Truce … hangry woman."

They chuckled.

He sat on the bed, along her right side, then pulled a candy bar from his pocket.

"You're so wrong for that." Cadence folded her arms, then stuck her tongue out at him. "But, it's cool."

A couple of taps on the door brought a smile to her face.

"Perfect timing," she said, shifting on the bed. "Come in."

"Hi." Steven poked his head inside.

The bewildered expression on Jackson's face matched the confusion in her head.

"Congratulations," he said, walking inside with a yellow and green decorated basket. "I wasn't sure if you had a boy or a girl."

"Thanks," Jackson countered, taking the gift and handing it to Cadence. "Our son's name is Caden."

The weaved basket was filled with diapers, baby wipes, washcloths, onesies, a baby rattle, and other items that she couldn't see on the bottom.

"This is very nice." Cadence motioned for Jackson to sit the basket on the side table. "How did you know I had the baby?"

"It was on the news—— the accident," Steven clarified. "I wasn't sure who the passengers were, but a witness said that it was a hit and run and that one of the victims was pregnant. The location wasn't too far from the courthouse, and when the camera zoomed in, I noticed the tire laying in the middle of the street had the custom-Adali emblem." He swallowed, taking a deep breath. "I knew it was you."

"That still doesn't answer my question."

"The news reported that they rushed the occupants to

Stroger Hospital. I came by the following day, and they gave me a visitor's pass to the maternity ward."

Cadence glanced at Steven.

"I wanted to make sure you were okay," he said, moving toward the foot of the bed. "I waited until today to give you a chance to get your bearings. I have two little ones now." Steven's shoulders relaxed, and a smile wider than the horizon over the ocean, split his face when he mentioned his children. "And I know childbirth can be stressful under the best of circumstances."

Cadence's guard deflated. No one was capable of faking the emotion that she witnessed.

"That's all I wanted." He rocked back on his heels. "I'll be going now. Take care."

"Hold on a minute," Cadence called out, glancing at her husband. "Have a seat."

Steven hesitated.

"Come on, man." Jackson nodded. "It's all good."

Steven walked to the other side of the room, pulled the recliner closer, and angled it in Cadence and Jackson's direction.

"This would be a good time to talk to you about Jackie," she suggested, just as a tap on the door interrupted her speaking.

"Hiiiiii, Cadence," Nurse Shannan said in a happy tone, not waiting for Cadence's verbal response to enter the room. "It's dinner time."

"Finally," she replied, doing a little dance.

Jackson raised from the bed, guiding the rolling table over for Shannan to place the tray. She smelled like fresh baby powder and was as cute as can be in Winnie-the-Pooh scrubs.

"Can I get you anything?" Shannan asked, checking the water pitcher.

"I'm good," Cadence responded, removing the lid, inhaling the aroma from the baked chicken, green beans, mashed potatoes with brown gravy, and a dinner roll.

"Enjoy, and let me know if you need anything else."

"Will do," she mumbled around a mouth filled with chicken.

Jackson grinned, crossing his arms, snickering. He leaned against the wall, then turned to Steven. "You know I'm not all that fond of you. I have reservations about you spending time with my daughter."

"I understand," Steven replied, scooting to the edge of the seat. "If it were reversed, I'd probably feel the same. The only thing I can tell you for certain is that I'm not the same man. So much has changed."

Cadence listened intently.

"I envied Braelyn, and with that came resentment. She grew up in the same house as our mom, but that's only because mother chose her, and she left me with our cruel father—— or should I say the man who raised me as his own. I didn't know at the time that we were the product of an affair."

Cadence knew this from the information her assistant, Jennifer, dug up on the Nevels family when Braelyn whirled into their life, causing more damage than a tornado.

"I looked like my mother, but Braelyn favored our biological father, and my father—— Simon, Irene's husband, couldn't accept that Irene's illegitimate daughter was the spitting image of her lover, the janitor." Steven sighed, picking the pretend lent from his jeans. "Everyone would know that she'd been sleeping around on him. Simon told Irene that he couldn't accept Braelyn as his own. So, she took Braelyn and left me behind."

"That's messed up," Jackson remarked, lifting a green bean from Cadence's plate, and she slapped his hand.

Steven laughed. "She's serious about that food."

"Hell yeah, I am," Cadence answered, spreading butter on the dinner roll. "I'm making up for missed meals."

"Again," Jackson said, pointing to the date on the dry-erase whiteboard of the day she was admitted. "Three days."

"Ain't nobody thinking about you." Cadence waved Jackson off and put her focus on Steven. "How did you end up helping Braelyn? She told me about Lester's plan and that she asked you. What made you do it?"

"Braelyn's my twin, and it was the first time I'd heard from her in six years," Steven said in a regretful tone, followed by an awkward silence. "We grew close over the long summers and weekends I'd spent at my mother's house. Even when I went away for college, we kept in contact. I'd send Braelyn money here and there cause she told me mom had her on a tight allowance, which I never understood—— she was loaded." Steven shrugged, sighing. "Anyway, our senior year, we were both home on spring break. One evening, I heard Braelyn and mother arguing. Next thing I know, Braelyn packed a bag and stormed out. Mom was cursing, saying she threw her life away and told me not to be like her. I didn't know what she meant. Later, I learned Braelyn had dropped out of college and off the face of the earth, forgetting about me in the process."

"That's a lot," Cadence sympathized, placing the fork on the tray, leaning back.

"I would've done anything to be close to her again. That doesn't make what I did right, but that's the truth." Steven stood and walked over to the window. "I didn't know Braelyn had a kid until she showed up at the Adali Global Reveal to get the VIP badge."

She felt sad for Steven. Cadence and her sister didn't talk every day, but she couldn't imagine Crystal disappearing from her life for years at a time.

"Simply put, I want to have a relationship with my niece and for my children to know their big cousin," Steven said, sliding a hand along the ledge. "Jackie's the only family I have left on my mother's side."

The reality of what he said, revealed that Irene had passed on to be with her Maker. No one but Steven's wife and kids in his world, though fulfilling, had to be a lonely life. Cadence knew it all too well; the four years they lived in Stuttgart, away from their entire family. Birthdays, school plays, Jackie learning to ride a bike, shared with their parents via FaceTime. It was something, but it was never enough. Steven didn't even have that.

Jackson glanced at Cadence, long enough for them to exchange a compassionate smile and a nod before he joined Steven by the window. "I don't see any harm in that. I think it would be good for Jackie to get to know her other side of the family, too."

Chapter 9

"There's no place like home," Cadence mumbled as Jackson parked in front of their house.

He let out a hearty chuckle. "You sound like Dorothy from the Wizard of Oz."

"Shut up." She giggled, slapping his arm. "You're comparing me to Judy Garland?"

"No," Jackson remarked; his eyebrows knitted as he smirked. "Diana Ross."

"That's The Wiz, *not* The Wizard of Oz, silly," Cadence chided him.

"Same difference."

"Not really."

"You keep correcting me," Jackson teased, his hand hovering over the steering wheel. "I may have to take you back to Stroger."

"You know you missed me."

"I guess." He jerked toward the driver's side door, glaring across at Cadence with an animated expression. "Let me quit playing," Jackson said, smiling at her. "It's been five days too long." He straightened himself, gliding a hand along her arm. "Being at the hospital with you every day isn't the same as having you home with me." He turned off the truck, then came around to open the door and assist Cadence.

"Mama Ceeeeeeeeeee," Jackie squealed, running down the stairs toward Cadence with her coat flapping like a cape.

"Slow down, sweetheart," Jackson grabbed her before she slammed into Cadence for a bear hug. "Mama's a little fragile right now."

"So, I can't hug her?" Jackie's asked, crossing her arms.

"Of course you can," Cadence interjected, sliding the purse strap on her shoulder. "But help daddy with the bags, and let's get in the house first."

"Okay," Jackie said, grabbing the yellow tote bag and a stuffed animal from the backseat. "Where's Caden?"

"At the hospital," Cadence replied while Jackson guided her up the stairs.

"Hey, darling," Phylicia greeted from the doorway, taking Cadence's purse. "Welcome home."

"Thanks, mom."

Once inside, Cadence inhaled the most savory aroma. "Is

that succotash?" she asked, turning to face her mother.

"Yes, dear," Phylicia replied. "Your great-great-great-grandmother's recipe."

"This makes me feel a little better after having to leave Caden there alone," Cadence mumbled, lowering on the couch, trying not to wince in front of Jackie.

The stitches on the left side of her abdomen pulled with every move she made.

"But, you know what will make me feel even better?"

"What's that?" Phylicia asked, placing a pillow behind Cadence's back.

"Is a hug from my favorite girl."

Jackie stood at a distance with her head hung low.

"I don't want to hurt you."

"Love never hurts." Cadence smiled and opened her arms wide. "For now, instead of big bear hugs, let's do baby bear hugs."

Jackie came forward and carefully laid her upper body on Cadence's chest. "I've missed you."

"Not more than I've missed you," Cadence responded, rubbing her back.

"Why did the baby have to stay at the hospital?" Jackie asked, perching on the arm of the couch. "Is he sick?"

"He was born early. The special doctors and nurses that work with tiny babies, have equipment there to help Caden get stronger until he's able to come home," Cadence explained, patting Jackie's knee. "You don't have to worry about him. He's being taken good care of, I promise."

A slow grin spread across Jackie's lips until her entire face beamed. "I can't wait to meet my little brother."

"You will soon," Cadence reassured her. "Tell me what you've been up to while I've been gone?"

Jackie hopped off the couch and ran across the living room to her daddy, who had just finished putting Cadence's things away. "Can I show her?"

Cadence looked back and forth from Jackson to Jackie. "Momma. What are they up to?"

"I don't know," Phylicia replied, but her tone revealed otherwise.

"Sure," Jackson said, and she rushed over to Cadence.

"Come on, Mama Cee." Jackie extended a hand to help Cadence to her feet. "Now close your eyes."

"I got you, baby." Jackson snaked an arm behind her back as they maneuvered through the house. "Take your time."

"No peeking," Jackie ordered.

Cadence saw the shadows behind her lids from someone waving their hands in front of her face. From the angle, she knew it was Jackie. They walked a few feet, turned right, then made a sharp left. The floor under her feet went from hardwood to plush softness. Her face twisted at the unfamiliar footing. Based on the way she was guided, Cadence knew she was in the guest bedroom, but it wasn't carpeted.

"Mama Cee, no peeking."

"I'm not," Cadence refuted, feeling a solid object pressed against the back of her knees.

"Sit," Jackson said, holding both of her hands. "I got you."

Cadence inhaled, enjoying the minty smell of Jackson's breath.

She lowered onto a soft cushion that hugged her body on all sides. It felt amazing.

"On the count of three, you can open your eyes," Jackie said in a cheerful tone. "One. Two. Three.

Cadence gasped at the beautiful sight before her, clasping her chest.

Charcoal grey walls, a white tree with mustard yellow leaves, and safari animal decals adorned the flat surface. The friendly lion, giraffe, and elephant stood tall while the three brown monkeys hung from the branches, smiling. Two fuzzy shaped, sunflower area rugs were placed inches apart on the wall-to-wall pickle green carpet.

"How?" she asked, admiring the crib, changing table, and chest of drawers, all in a smooth white wooden finish. "When did you have the time to do this?"

Jackson rubbed the back of his head. "I had some——"

"Uncle Steven helped us," Jackie blurted out.

"Did he?" Cadence remarked, angling a glance at her husband.

"Me, Stevie Junior, and Amber picked out the animals," Jackie boasted, swinging from side to side, and her blonde curly tresses followed.

"You guys did a terrific job," Cadence praised, walking over and opening the drawers. They were stocked with baby wipes, lotion, and butt cream. "I'm still in awe."

Jackson stepped behind Cadence, wrapping his arms

around her chest, and kissed the spot behind her ear. A tingling warmth traveled from her hair follicles down to her lilac toenails that were in desperate need of a pedicure.

Cadence turned her head to meet the tender lips that trailed her cheekbone. She closed her eyes as Jackson laid a lingering peck on her mouth.

Click. Click. Click.

"Oooooo, daddy," Jackie snickered, leaning her head against Cadence's side.

Click. Click. Click.

Cadence's eyes opened, landing on Phylicia standing in the doorway with a camera lifted in front of her face.

"Momma," Cadence said, tilting her head, resting it on Jackson's chest. "How long have you been taking pictures?"

Phylicia lowered the camera in front of her bosom. "Long enough to capture all the special moments," she replied, lifting the camera again. "Caden will know how much he's loved from day one."

Click. Click. Click.

"He's gonna need to see his granny in some of these," Cadence shot back. "Can't you put that on a timer and hop in here with us?"

"Sure can," she said, propping the camera on the chest of drawers.

The doorbell chimed the familiar tune of Beethoven 5th throughout the house.

Phylicia turned, facing Cadence and Jackson. "Are y'all expecting anyone?"

"No," Jackson replied, then glanced at Cadence.

"Definitely not," she protested, rubbing her belly out of habit. "I wasn't even sure I was getting discharged today. No one knows I'm home."

"Daddy," Jackie yelled, her voice further away than it should be.

Cadence was baffled. She hadn't realized that Jackie had left the nursery.

"Uncle Steven's here."

Chapter 10

"Hey Steven," Jackson said, giving him a thorough once-over. "I'm surprised to see you."

"Sorry for dropping in unannounced," he responded, stepping into the living room as Jackie dashed around him, looking out the door.

"Where's Stevie Junior and Amber?" she asked, moving to the window and peering under the bamboo blinds. "Why didn't you bring them with you?"

"They're still at daycare." Steven smiled, glancing over at his niece. "Maybe I'll bring them by later if it's okay with your dad."

Jackie stared at Jackson with expecting eyes.

"Not today, sweetheart. Your mom just got home, and she needs rest."

"We'll be quiet. I promise."

"Nice try, but another day," Jackson said, and she sighed, scurrying to the back at the sound of Phylicia calling her name.

"I didn't know Cadence, and the baby were discharged."

"Just Cadence," Jackson corrected, rubbing his chin. "Caden will be in the NICU for a few more weeks until he gets stronger."

"Don't worry. Babies are resilient. He's going to come out of there stronger than ever."

"Caden's a fighter. He's already proven that by surviving the accident," Jackson said, making a tight fist and nodded, thinking about his baby boy. "We're blessed. The pediatrician said he might have slight complications because of the early delivery, but I welcome all of it. The alternative would have been so much worse."

"True," Steven agreed, digging in his coat pocket and plucking out the car keys. "We can do this at another time." He turned on the soles of his sneakers toward the front door.

"Hold up," Jackson countered, grabbing his shoulder. "You didn't come over here for no reason."

"I wanted to run something by you, but it can wait."

"Apparently not, if you made a special trip. What has you on edge?" Jackson asked, examining the worry lines in Steven's forehead and the tightness in his jawbone. "I can see whatever it is has you disturbed by the stress in your face."

"Thank you so much for helping decorate the nursery. It's beautiful," Cadence called out as she walked into the room, causing the men to stop talking and turn in her direction.

"It was my pleasure."

"Did I catch you two in the middle of something?" she asked, moving in closer.

Steven appeared as if he'd been caught with his pants down behind the bleachers making out with a girl. His cheeks flushed pink, and his mouth opened, but no words were spoken. At that moment, Jackson knew that whatever Steven had to say, he didn't want to say it in Cadence's presence.

"He came by to drop off the spare key I'd given him while we were working on the nursery," Jackson lied, grabbing his house keys from the end table, then lifting a hoodie from the coat rack. "I'm going to walk Steven out."

"Welcome home," Steven said, finally recovering from the temporary impairment. "Get as much rest as possible. Your days of sleeping through the night are numbered."

"So I've been told," Cadence responded, trying to stifle a yawn. "I guess I need to get on that pronto."

The three of them chuckled.

"Tell Jackie I said goodbye, and when you feel up to it, I'll bring the kids over," Steven said right before walking out of the door.

Once they got to Steven's car, Jackson glanced over and said, "Let's go for a drive."

"Okay."

Jackson lowered into the two-seater, Adali G8, admiring

the chrome and black leather interior. Adali vehicles smelled like money, and Steven's sports model wasn't any different.

"This definitely isn't the family car," Jackson commented, grazing his fingers along the soft leather dashboard.

"This is my baby, Vesta." Steven grinned, rolling his palm over the steering wheel. "The only girl who gets as much attention as my wife, Deb, who by the way, can't wait to meet your family."

"I feel you on that."

"One of the many perks of working for Adali Automotive." Steven beamed, starting the vehicle with keyless ignition. "But I don't have to tell you that."

Jackson fastened the seatbelt as Steven pulled away from the curb. Though he wanted to ask Steven why he came by, Jackson fought the instinct and gave him a chance to regain his nerve. Nothing like a drive to refocus a person's thoughts.

After ten minutes of driving down Pulaski Road, Steven turned down the radio and said, "I don't think your car accident was an accident at all.

Jackson wasn't expecting to hear that.

"I believed this when I visited Cadence in the hospital, but I couldn't put that on her, especially after I learned she had the baby. And before you ask." Steven raised his hand. "I didn't say anything at the house while we were putting the nursery together because the children were always around. My kids are young and wouldn't understand, but Jackie would, and she didn't need to overhear that someone tried to kill her parents."

Jackson listened in silence as he absorbed the gravity of

Steven's words.

"When I came to the hospital, squad cars and news crews from all the major stations flooded the parking lot. It was a spectacle. The police were keeping reporters from entering the building. Even ADA Knox was there."

"Why would he be there?" Jackson whipped his head in Steven's direction.

"I don't know," Steven said, pulling into the grocery store parking lot and retrieving his phone from the cupholder. "I saved the footage from the police camera on the corner of Twenty-Sixth and Western from the day of the accident."

"How do you have that?"

"It was on the news," Steven replied, scrolling through his phone. "Not when the accident was first reported, but the following morning. Channel seven aired the footage from the street camera. Three people approached the car to help, but the news only interviewed two of them."

"I remember someone else being there, but I couldn't see him," Jackson remarked, reflecting on the events of that day. "Maybe he left the scene before the police arrived."

"There's a reason the man disappeared when he did," Steven said, angling the phone toward Jackson. "Look at this."

Jackson inwardly cringed, watching the eighteen-wheeler barrel toward them on the wrong side of the road. His life flashed before him that day. The only other time he'd been that scared was when he called the police station to check on Cadence after Detective O'Brien took her in for questioning, following Braelyn's murder.

* * *

Cadence had gone by Braelyn's house to check on her safety. Jackson and Cadence offered Braelyn refuge at their home until she found a place, far away from Lester. When Cadence arrived, she heard the commotion on the other side of the front door. She called out to Braelyn and checked the knob, which was unlocked. Cadence entered just as someone fled the scene through the rear door. Braelyn laid in a pool of blood, clutching a gun, gasping for the last breaths she would ever take.

* * *

Nothing about the video seemed peculiar. Jackson continued to observe as a man; then, a woman ran over to what was left of the driver's side of the vehicle.

Steven placed two fingers on the screen and spread them apart, enlarging the image as the third witness came over, who stood in front of the car.

"Do you know who that is?" Steven asked, glancing at Jackson. "Did you see him?"

"I couldn't from my angle," Jackson replied, focusing on the image. "I was lying on top of Cadence, so my back was to the windshield," he said, glaring harder at the screen. "I remember he said something and——"

"What?" Steven asked; anticipation dripped from his tone.

"Cadence had blacked-out," Jackson recalled, folding his arms. "I couldn't get her to wake up. But then, somebody said something, and Cadence's eyes opened." He looked at Steven. "I think she was trying to tell me something, but I was just thrilled that she woke up, and I missed it."

"She recognized his voice."

"Whose?"

"Detective O'Brien."

Chapter 11

"How's that even possible?" Jackson asked, taking the phone from Steven and rewinding the clip. "He's in lock-up until trial."

"No, he isn't," Steven countered. "He's out on bond."

Jackson's stomach churned in disgust. "This is a criminal case. How's he roaming free?"

"Up until now, his record was clean … at least on paper," Steven remarked with a smirk that mirrored Jackson's feelings. "No flight risk, pillar of the community, etcetera, etcetera."

"Crooked ass police department strikes again." Jackson huffed, examining the video.

Detective O'Brien on the streets was an added concern that his family didn't need. Jackson made a mental note to contact Sly and Tony to tell them about this new development.

"How can you be so sure that it's him?" Jackson said, giving the phone back to Steven. "The man never turns around."

"That skullcap," he shot back, sounding sure of himself.

"It's a winter hat." Jackson shrugged, glancing at Steven. "I see nothing special about it."

Steven manipulated the video, freezing it on the back of the man's head, then zooming in as far as he could without making the image blurry.

"You see that checkerboard design?" Steven pointed at the screen. "That's standard police department issued."

"It's red. Shouldn't it be black and white?"

"Precisely," Steven fired back. "The cops on Lester's payroll wore skullcaps with embroidered red and black checkerboard, minus the police star decal. It's barely noticeable from a distance."

"How do you know this?"

"I overheard Braelyn talking to Lester about it when they were plotting to extort Cadence at the Adali Global Event," Steven admitted, shifting his focus out of the window. "The look was subtle but noticeable enough to those who knew what it represented."

"So, you're saying that you believe this man is Detective O'Brien or one of his twisted cop friends?"

"Yes."

Jackson marinated on that for a moment. He touched

Steven's shoulder, making him avert his attention back in Jackson's direction. "Cadence can't know about this. She already has enough to deal with without this added stressor."

Steven nodded. "Now what?"

"Take me back to the house before Cadence starts to worry," Jackson replied, scrolling through his phone. "I'm going to give ADA Knox a call."

Twenty minutes later, Steven double-parked in front of Jackson's home.

"Thanks for telling me this," Jackson said, zipping the hoodie up to his collarbone. "I appreciate it more than you know."

"You're welcome. If I learn anything else, you'll be the first to know."

Jackson opened the door just as a series of rapid knocks tapped against Steven's window.

"Steven Bekker," a man called out wearing a plaid tweed coat with a beard longer and fuller than James Harden of the Houston Rockets.

"Yes," Steven responded, cracking the window.

"You've been served," he said, sliding a manila envelope through the small opening.

Jackson closed the door, shifting his complete focus to Steven.

"What the hell is this?" Steven mumbled, glancing out the window. The man had vanished just as fast as he appeared.

Jackson watched with great anticipation as Steven tore open the envelope and pulled out papers that resembled court documents.

"This can't be real," Steven seethed, tossing the papers on the dashboard.

"What is it?"

"I'm being called to testify for the *defense*."

Jackson shuddered. "This is the day that just keeps on giving bullshit on top of bullshit."

"I'm not sure what the angle is, but I'm positive the defense has one," Steven commented, running his palms down his face. "I don't have any connection to Detective O'Brien."

"But you do to Lester," Jackson refuted, grabbing the papers and looking them over. "Maybe they're linking them together."

"But why?" Steven asked, gripping the steering wheel. "Lester could be in Mexico for all we know. No one's heard or seen him since …" Steven's chin dropped to his chest. "He killed my sister."

"Did you want to come in for a minute?" Jackson asked, assessing the distress in Steven's body language.

"No. I'll be alright," he replied, checking the rearview mirror. "You go ahead inside, take care of Cadence, and do what you need to do."

"Are you sure?"

"Positive," Steven said, looking in the side mirror. "I have to move the car anyway; there's a truck approaching."

Soon as Jackson exited and closed the door, Steven peeled away as if he were being chased. Jackson scanned the area as a precaution before heading into the house. He knew Sly and

Tony, or one of their trusted associates, were observing from the shadows. That gave him some comfort.

"Shhhh," Phylicia said, placing a finger to her lips as Jackson closed the front door.

She was stretched out on the couch with Jackie tucked into the groove of her hip on the inner part of the sofa.

"Jackie just nodded off." Phylicia smiled, rotating her neck. "She was hoping you'd change your mind about the kids coming over."

"Sounds like her," Jackson replied, grinning at his sleeping daughter. "Where's Cadence?"

"Finally, resting."

"That's good."

"It is," Phylicia agreed; her voice tinged with sadness. "She's missing Caden. I tried to get her to lie down in the bedroom, but she insisted on staying in the nursery. She said she felt closer to Caden in there."

"Oh, my." Jackson's head lowered as his heart ached for his wife. He felt helpless.

"I couldn't argue with her. I don't know what it's like to give birth and have to leave your baby behind. I made sure the chair was in a reclining position and covered her up," Phylicia said, extending a hand toward Jackson. "Come here, son."

He moved forward, lowered to his knees, and took her hand.

"You take care of my daughter," she said, gazing into Jackson's eyes. "In order to do that, you must take care of yourself. You'll get through all of this together, you hear me."

"Loud and clear, mama," he replied, kissing the back of her hand. "I'm going to put Jackie in bed so you can get some rest."

"I appreciate that."

Jackson carried Jackie upstairs to her room, then peeked in on Cadence. An angel itself couldn't have appeared more at peace than she did at that moment. He was so grateful to his mother-in-law for being the caring woman she was, and for always looking out for their best interest. Jackson loved Phylicia just as much as he loved his own mother.

He retired to the bedroom, retrieved Cadence's phone, and scrolled through the contacts until he found ADA Knox's number.

"Hello, Mrs. Goldsmith."

"Not Mrs.," he corrected, surprised by how quick Knox answered. "It's Jackson."

"My apologies," Knox said. "Cadence's number came across the caller ID. I assumed you were her. Is everything okay?"

"Not really," Jackson replied, sitting on the bed. "But before I say anything, you need to promise me that this stays between us."

"Jackson, I can't give you that assurance until I hear what you have to say," Knox retorted. "If you're about to confess to a crime, I suggest you speak with an attorney."

"I haven't committed a crime," Jackson shot back.

"Then we shouldn't have any problems."

"Cadence can't know what I'm about to tell you."

"Alright," he responded in a concerned tone. "She won't hear anything from me."

"Thank you," Jackson uttered, releasing a heavy sigh. "I'm just trying to protect her the best way I know how," he said, clearing his throat, then whispered, "I believe Detective O'Brien was behind our car accident."

"So do I."

Jackson damn near dropped the phone.

"I need absolute proof before I can bring it to the court."

"Did you see the footage from the accident?"

"Yes. It's not enough and can be easily disputed since Detective O'Brien never shows his face to the camera," Knox said. "It would be our word against his."

"What about the witnesses?" Jackson inquired, thinking back to that day. "They got a good look at him."

"I'd rather not involve innocent civilians; besides, I have someone on the case."

"Can you trust this person?" Jackson asked with legit skepticism. "My faith in law enforcement is cellophane thin."

"He's the best," Knox responded; a confident air was in his tone. "Detective Xavier Carter is my go-to guy, especially when infiltrating gangs and dirty cops. He knows how to stay under the radar and can adapt to any situation. He reports to me, and only me, regarding this investigation."

"That's good," Jackson whispered, walking the length of the short hall, and peeking into the nursery to see if Cadence was still asleep. He pulled the door closed, then reentered his bedroom. "Again, between you and me. My wife can never know that asshole tried to kill us."

80 London St. Charles

know that asshole tried to kill us."

Chapter 12

"Long time, no hear," Cadence said into the receiver, closing the laptop. "What's it been … three weeks?"

"Unfortunately," Knox replied with an uneasy chuckle. "And I believe the phrase is long time, no see."

"I know what I said," she shot back, pushing the laptop away from the edge and placing her elbows on the kitchen table. "Please tell me you're calling with good news."

"Well …"

"That doesn't sound promising."

"I finally have access to my office."

"Why didn't you lead with that?" Cadence chided him. "That's great news."

"I wish it was," Knox countered. "I can't help but feel hoodwinked." He paused for a moment. "It took them three weeks to turn up nothing. No fingerprints. No evidence. The security cameras were scrubbed clean. Nothing."

Cadence's head dropped into the palm of her hands.

"This was merely a stall tactic on the crime scene investigator's part," Knox remarked in a low voice. "The order had to come from the top of the food chain."

"But why?"

"We're going after corruption in the police department," Knox explained. "It's too soon after the Van Dyke case. They want this to go away."

"What does that mean for me?" Cadence asked, lifting her head. "I don't get the justice I deserve. Braelyn's murder goes unsolved and the detective that helped orchestrate the cover-up, gets off unscathed?"

"I know this is frustrating, but don't give up on me," Knox pleaded. "We have one week left."

"Fuck this shit." She banged the table with her fist. "I brought my family back here and put them in danger, for what?"

"Hang with me, Cadence," Knox implored. "Are you still willing to testify?"

"Yes."

"Mama Cee, come on," Jackie said, running into the kitchen. "You said I could go see Caden today."

"One minute, Jackie," she responded, covering the phone. "Go finish up your room, and then we'll be on our way."

Jackie gave Cadence a quick peck on the cheek, then ran

down the hall and stomped up the stairs.

"You take care of your family and baby Caden," Knox said. "I'll be in touch. I have some investigating of my own to do."

"I can't believe this shit." Cadence fumed, disconnecting the call and sliding the phone across the kitchen table.

"What happened?" Jackson asked, rounding the corner and entering the room in a pair of basketball shorts and a soaked tank top with a towel draped over his shoulder.

"After all this time, Knox was let back into his office, only to be in a worse predicament than when he started the investigation." Cadence leaned back into the chair. "We have nothing."

"I don't know what to say," Jackson said, peeling off the tank top, and wiping his face, neck, and chest with the towel.

"I'm so mad I could cry."

Jackson walked over and kneaded her shoulders. "Something's going to turn up. It just has to."

"I hope you're right." Cadence sighed, resting her head against Jackson's washboard abs.

He bent over and kissed her lips. "I'm about to jump in the shower so that we can get out of here. You wanna join me?"

"Why do you keep torturing yourself?" she teased, reaching back and squeezing Jackson's firm behind. "It's only been three weeks, Sir. You still can't have none."

"I know," he whined, sliding his hands over her breasts. "But that doesn't mean I can't pleasure you."

"Jackie will never meet her little brother if we do that."

"I'll be quick," Jackson countered, his tone throaty and heavy.

"The lies you tell." Cadence grinned, pushing him back so she could touch his manhood. "You're already aroused."

Jackson's eyes pleaded with hers.

Cadence stood, then glanced toward the kitchen entryway as she backed Jackson into the walk-in pantry. She closed the door, positioning him against it, then slid his shorts down until they pooled around his ankles.

Five minutes later, Jackson was singing her name off-key, holding onto the shelves while struggling to remain on his feet.

She fixed his shorts, then went on her tippy-toes and kissed him. "You good?" she asked, nibbling his bottom lip.

"Mmmm hmmm," he groaned, gazing at her with hooded eyes. "You're the best."

"I know," she purred, licking her lips. "Now, go take your shower."

Jackson hadn't gotten out of the kitchen good, before Cadence flipped open her laptop, retrieved the phone, and called Steven.

"Hi, Cadence," Steven answered in a chipper voice. "I'm surprised to hear from you. Is Jackie nagging you as much as my kids are hounding me about getting together?"

"She's been eager to spend time with them again," Cadence said, opening the company email. "We're all family, and she needs to know you and her cousins better, as well as your wife."

"They did hit it off pretty well while we decorated the

nursery," he replied. "Deb brought us food every day during her lunch break. She loves Jackie just as much as I do. Maybe we can set up a play date at Odyssey Fun World or take them bowling, all of us as a family."

"That can be arranged once I'm up and moving about. I spend my days at the hospital with Caden."

"How's he doing?"

"Great," Cadence said, and she could feel the corners of her lips turn upward in a smile. "He's gained a pound and is eating about three ounces every three to four hours. The doctors are happy with his progress."

"That's fantastic."

Cadence scrolled through old work emails. "Hey—— can you send me the quarterly earnings for the downtown office?"

"Aren't you on maternity leave?"

"Yeahhhhhh …"

Steven was so quiet that Cadence could hear his thoughts.

"Technically, I'm on leave, that's why I can't access any current files."

If it weren't for Steven's name and the running timer on the screen to let Cadence know they were still connected, she would've thought he'd hung up.

"Full disclosure," Cadence confessed, scanning through saved emails from four years ago. "I just learned that the ADA's case against Detective O'Brien is blown, and I need something to keep me busy before I lose my mind."

"Okay." He let out a deep sigh. "I'll send them to my personal email, then forward it to you."

The phone slipped from Cadence's hands and slammed onto the table. She rapidly pressed the volume button, then clutched both sides of the laptop and pulled the screen to her ear.

Triumphant tears poured from her eyes.

"I'm ready," Jackie burst into the kitchen. "Let's go."

"Um." She closed the laptop and placed it on the table. "Daddy's going to take you," Cadence said, wiping her face.

"I thought we were going as a family?" Jackie frowned.

"We are," Jackson said, putting on his coat, glancing over at Cadence.

"Babe— I'll meet you there."

"Go get your coat and wait by the front door," Jackson instructed, playfully tugging Jackie's ponytail. "I need to talk to mommy."

Cadence smiled at Jackie, disappointed that she had to break her daughter's heart.

Soon as she was out of earshot, Jackson asked, "What's going on? You know she's been looking forward to this for weeks."

"Listen." Cadence opened the laptop and played the recording.

Jackson ran a hand across his waves. "Is that Detective O'Brien?"

She nodded.

"I didn't know I still had this," Cadence explained, grabbing her phone and realized that Steven was still on the line. "Disregard. I'll call you later."

"Who was that?"

"It doesn't matter." She waved him off, disconnecting the call. "I need to get this to Knox."

"We can do it on our way back from visiting Caden," Jackson suggested.

"No," she argued, sliding the phone in her pocket and gripping the laptop. "I need to do this now. The office will be closed by the time we're done."

Jackson glared at Cadence; his lips formed a hard line.

"Please don't look at me like that. I promise I'll be there as soon as I'm done," she assured, retrieving four bottles of breastmilk from the refrigerator and handing them to Jackson.

"We'll be waiting," Jackson replied, pecking Cadence on the cheek. "Don't let her down."

"I won't," she promised, touching his chest. "Thanks for understanding."

"Let's hit it, baby girl," Jackson said as he walked toward the front of the house.

Cadence took a deep breath, checked the time, then called Knox.

"Assistant District Attorney, Aaron Knox speaking."

How long are you going to be in your office?"

"May I ask with whom I'm speaking?"

"It's Cadence. Cadence Goldsmith."

"Slow down, Cadence," he said, clearing this throat. "Is everything alright?"

"How long are you going to be in your office?" she asked again.

"I was on my way out."

"Don't go anywhere," she demanded, snatching her keys from the counter. "I'm on my way."

Chapter 13

Cadence drove north, opposite of the rush hour traffic toward the Loop, shaving ten minutes off of what would've been a thirty-minute commute. She pulled into the expensive parking garage, grabbed her belongings, then hopped out of her vehicle.

The moment she exited the garage, Cadence stepped into a pool of businessmen and women in suits, heels, briefcases, and AirPods in their ears, moving with a purpose. The atmosphere was all too familiar. Adali Automotive office was two blocks north of the Dirksen Federal Building, where Knox's office was located.

She strategically maneuvered amongst the people, jogging across the street, wincing with every bounce. Although she's three weeks postpartum, Cadence had a long way to go before she was completely healed.

Rushing through the revolving glass door, she placed her bag, coat, and purse on the conveyor belt and walked through the body scanner. Cadence anticipated the censor beeping since that seemed to be the new norm whenever she entered a county or federal building, but it hadn't. Maybe that didn't occur because this was an impromptu visit.

She rushed to the elevator and pressed the button for the ninth floor.

Her heart raced on the ride up, and it had nothing to do with the exertion from running. Doubt crept into her mind. This was the very place where all the evidence did a Houdini. Maybe she should have asked Knox to meet her somewhere else.

The chime pulled Cadence from her thoughts. She clutched the bag at her side as the steel doors slid open.

"Good afternoon," she said to the beefy young man with a low fade, sitting behind the information desk. "I have an appointment with ADA Knox."

"Your name?" he asked, scanning her from head to toe.

She mentally rolled her eyes. Cadence didn't want to say who she was. No one needed to know she was there.

"Ms. Goldsmith," she said, glancing down at his name tag. "Rowan, I don't have an official appointment, but he is expecting me."

He glanced up at Cadence, then reached for the phone. "I

have a Ms. Goldsmith here to see you."

She hoped this wasn't a mistake.

"Yes, sir," Rowan said, then placed the phone on the base. "He'll be right with you."

"Thanks," Cadence replied, moving toward the window, admiring the skyscrapers, and daydreaming about simpler times.

"Ms. Goldsmith," Knox called out, moving toward her. "It's good to see you."

"Thanks for allowing me to come in on such short notice," Cadence said, shocked by his relaxed appearance, in a pair of black joggers with a matching hoodie and bleached-white sneakers.

"It's not like you gave me much choice," he countered, giving her a side-eye. "Walk with me."

They traveled down a long corridor, stopping in front of a door, manned by two armed guards. Knox pulled a key from his pocket and unlocked the deadbolt.

"After you," he said, gesturing for Cadence to enter.

Knox closed and secured the door, leaving the key in the lock.

She gave the office a thorough once-over. "This looks much different than before."

"After what happened, I spared no expense," Knox whispered, leaning in close. "I even installed my own private security cameras that I can access remotely." He removed an oversized gym bag from the chair in front of his desk. "Please, have a seat."

Cadence pulled the laptop from her bag, balanced it on her lap, then flipped it open. "I was going through old emails and found this," she said, pressing the play button: *Whatever you think you know about what happened today, you better have fucking amnesia tomorrow when you speak with Officer Douglas. Do I make myself clear? Good. If you're feeling brave in the morning, just remember, I know where you live.*

Knox's eyeballs bulged from their sockets as he jumped, pumping his fist in the air. "We got him."

She shared Knox's enthusiasm. It was time for Detective O'Brien to go down.

"Send this to my personal email," he instructed, scribbling the address on a yellow legal pad. "I can't chance anything coming through here."

"Gotcha."

"This was undeniably worth missing my pick-up game with the guys," Knox commented, opening the email on his phone. "I got it." He paused, glancing at Cadence. "This will all be over soon."

"At least this part," Cadence muttered. "Lester's still out there."

"It's just a matter of time until he's caught," Knox reassured her. "I can guarantee you; O'Brien will flip on Lester to save his own ass. He'll use him as a bargaining chip for a reduced sentence."

"I hope you're right," she countered, closing the laptop and placing it in her tote.

Knox nodded, grabbing his gym bag. "Come on. I'll ride

down with you."

* * *

Cadence put her things in the backseat, then texted Jackson to let him know she was on the way to the hospital. She started the engine but didn't put the car into gear. Resting her head on the steering wheel, Cadence released a sigh. She couldn't shake the eerie feeling that washed over her. Maybe it was all the talk about Lester and scummy O'Brien.

She put on her Ledisi playlist and cranked the volume. Nothing like soulful crooning to drown out negative feelings.

Even though she was in the heart of rush hour, it didn't take Cadence too long to make it to Stroger Hospital. She parked in the dimly lit lot and rushed into the main entrance.

"How're you doing tonight?" asked the woman whose face always looked like she was about to model for a professional photoshoot.

"Great, Keshia," Cadence replied, waiting while she wrote her name on a visitor's pass to the NICU.

"Here you go," Keshia offered a warm smile. "As always, I'm praying for the day when I don't see you on the regular unless you're bringing that sweet baby to visit me."

"Same," Cadence replied, taking the pass. "Enjoy the rest of your night."

Her inner spirit was at peace. The music played its part, but not as much as the feeling that coursed through her, the closer she got to spending time with Caden. She and Jackson were fortunate. Caden was faring well, and there had been talk about him coming home in the next couple of weeks. Some families would never have that chance. Cadence was there the night a baby born two days after Caden, had passed away. The heartbroken mother's wrenching shrills still haunted her.

Cadence stood outside the NICU, observing Jackie sitting on her daddy's lap with her hand inside the incubator while Jackson read, *Goodnight Moon*. Her heart exploded into a million happy pieces. She quickly took out her phone, zoomed in, and snapped a picture.

"Hi, mom," Nurse Martha whispered. "Would you like me to take a photo of the whole family?"

Martha always smelled like fresh baby powder. She had been caring for Caden from the very start, and was the one who reassured Cadence that her son would be okay. She felt more like family than some of her own relatives.

"I thought only two people at a time were allowed," Cadence countered, gazing at her family.

"True, but it's a slow night," she replied, taking Cadence's purse from her arms. "And it's almost feeding time." Martha paused, and a smile split her cocoa face. "Would you like to feed your son?"

"What?" Cadence's hand flew to her chest. "I get to hold him?"

"Yes."

She was overwhelmed with so much emotion that she couldn't speak.

Martha helped Cadence out of her coat, then said, "Here's a gown. You can disrobe in the changing room. Remove your shirt and bra, and wear the gown opened to the front," she advised. "Wash your hands and have a seat with your family. We're going to try skin-to-skin contact before Caden's feeding."

"Okay."

Five minutes later, Cadence joined Jackson and Jackie.

"Hey, honey," he greeted, rising to his feet, offering Cadence the recliner closest to the baby.

"I get to hold and feed him," she beamed, pulling the gown closed.

"Martha said I could hold him," Jackson replied, gazing into her eyes. "But I wanted you to be the first."

God, I love this man.

"Mama Cee, Caden squeezed my finger when I put my hand inside and started talking to him," Jackie chimed in. "I love him so much."

"Of course he did," Cadence replied, taking in Jackie's excitement. "He knows who you are."

"How's that?"

"Because he knows the sound of your voice."

Martha and another nurse retrieved Caden from the incubator, carefully maneuvering all of the tubes and wires. They placed him on Cadence's chest and pulled her gown over his back so that he wouldn't get cold. His heart beating against hers gave Cadence a great feeling that she couldn't put into words, but she loved every moment.

Jackson hovered over them and gently rubbed Caden's

head with two fingers, and Jackie laid on Cadence's shoulder, gazing at her little brother.

When it came time to feed him, Caden latched on, on the third try.

"Look at this little overachiever," Martha teased, showing Cadence the proper way to support him while breastfeeding.

"This is what we were all hoping to see," Dr. Garrison added, standing beside the incubator.

Cadence was so enthralled with her son that she didn't notice her presence.

"I take it this is a good thing?" Jackson asked, his voice slightly hitched.

"Yes," Dr. Garrison remarked. "If he keeps this up, Caden will be able to go home in the next couple of weeks."

* * *

"How did it go with Knox?" Jackson asked, escorting Cadence to her car.

"Let's just say I'm looking forward to the trial again," she responded.

"That good, huh?" Jackson remarked, opening Cadence's door, and she slid behind the wheel. She drove him five rows over to his truck.

Soon as Jackson opened the door, Jackie climbed out of the backseat.

"Hey," Cadence shouted, lifting her hands in the air.

"You're not staying with me?"

"I'm going to ride with daddy," Jackie fired back. "But just this time."

"That's cool. I see how it is."

"I'll follow you, Speedy Gonzalez." Jackson snickered, pressing the key fob. Jackie clambered into the backseat. "Don't leave us."

"Whatever." She shrugged, adjusting the rearview mirror. "You better keep up."

Cadence counted to ten, giving Jackie enough time to fasten her seatbelt, then took off. They always competed to see who'd beat the other one home, of course, without being reckless. She was driving the prototype she designed, the Adali SLX autonomous car, and Jackson had a new Adali G-Class truck since his vehicle was totaled in the accident.

She switched the playlist to 2Pac and hit it. Jackson was right behind her. She threw the peace sign out of the sunroof, then drove down the on-ramp to the Dan Ryan Expressway. Much to her surprise, Jackson got off three exits early.

What is he up to?

Cadence turned down the music to call Jackson, pausing when she heard movement behind her. She pressed the button, and the dome light came on. Checking the rearview mirror, she didn't see anything. Slowing down just a bit, Cadence felt behind the passenger's seat without taking her eyes off the road. Her laptop had fallen out of the bag.

Shifting in the seat, Cadence adjusted the seatbelt. "Call Jackson Goldsmith," she said out loud, and Siri dialed his number.

"Yessssss," he answered.

"Where'd you dip off to?" she asked and heard Jackie giggling in the background. "What's so funny, Jacqueline Nevels?"

"Nothing."

Cadence swerved around the curve between Wentworth and the Ninety-Ninth and Halsted exit with ease. "Jackson."

"If you must know," he said in a playful tone. "We're stopping at Baskin Robbins."

"What?" she frowned, coming off the ramp, and making a sharp left on Halsted. "She hasn't even had dinner yet."

"I promised Jackie we'd get ice cream after leaving the hospital."

"Mmmm hmmm," Cadence remarked. "That's why you put me down, huh?"

Jackie tittered in the background. "A promise is a promise."

Cadence grinned. She couldn't argue with that.

"Make sure a pint of pralines and cream finds its way home with y'all."

"Yes, dear," Jackson said, laughing. "See you soon."

Less than ten minutes later, Cadence had pulled in front of the house and turned off the engine. She lowered her chin to her chest and inhaled. Caden's sweet scent was still on her skin. She closed her eyes, basking in the joy she experienced, holding him for the first time.

Cadence got out of the car, scanned her surroundings, then opened the rear door, kneeling on the seat with her head down to retrieve the laptop from the floor. She used the flashlight on her phone to see if anything else had spilled from the bag. A few pens, sticky notes, and a pack of gum were scattered on the floor mats.

Leaning further into the car, that same eerie feeling returned, halting her movement. She slowly lifted her head, shining the flashlight out of the side and front windows. She didn't see anything. Cadence angled the light out of the back window only to be greeted by her trunk standing at attention. Just for a second, Cadence thought she'd hit the key fob by mistake, releasing the latch. She whipped her head toward the front, placing the light on the base of the steering wheel. The sight of the dangling keys sank Cadence's heart to the pit of her stomach.

"Surprise, bitch."

Chapter 14

"Get off of me!" Cadence screamed to the top of her lungs, kicking and clawing at the assailant. "Hellllllllp."

"I've been waiting for this moment," the man said, his tone gruff, grabbing her legs. He tried to yank her out of the car, but Cadence held onto the seat with all of her might.

When he realized that he wasn't getting anywhere, he climbed on top of her, putting a hand over her mouth. She bit down hard, snatched the mask off of his face, gripped the phone in her hand, and shined the light in his eyes.

Instantly, he drew a forearm to his face while trying to swipe the phone away with his free hand.

"Somebody help me," Cadence yelled into the night, trying to get a clear look at the guy.

Just as he drew his fist back to strike her, the weight of his body lifted from hers. She dug her heels into the cushion, pushing her body further into the car, fumbling to unlock the phone to dial 911.

"Hold his ass," a voice ordered that sounded all too familiar.

"Sly," she said under her breath, lowering the phone.

Cadence climbed out of the rear passenger door, clutching the left side of her stomach. She couldn't believe her eyes. Jackson's twin cousins, Sly and Tony, dressed in black leather, were pounding the shit out of … *Lester*.

She stood in shock for what felt like minutes but were probably only several seconds. Walking around to the trunk, she saw chip and candy bar wrappers strewn about, as well as a half-empty Gatorade bottle. *How long had he been in there?*

Lester's head was bald, and he was clean-shaven, much different from the cornrows and goatee he used to wear, and he seemed slimmer than before.

Cadence scanned the area above; though subtle, she noticed the slight movement from the blinds and curtains of her neighbors. They witnessed the attack or, at the very least, knew something had happened. Folks were afraid to get involved. Cadence understood that logic, but to ignore her cries for help … *Where did Sly and Tony come from? They live on the other side of town.*

Bright headlights beamed in their direction, breaking

Cadence from her thoughts.

"Oh, no, no, no," she whispered, spotting the Adali emblem on the hood of the truck. "Jackie doesn't need to see this."

Jackson swerved the nose of the truck into the spot behind Cadence's car and jumped out. The vehicle was still running. "You okay?" he asked, rushing to her side. "I'm alright."

"Take Jackie inside," he shouted, then ran up on Lester. "You fucking with my wife?" Jackson growled, punching him in the mouth, then the stomach.

"Jackson, no," Cadence screamed.

It felt like déjà vu.

Four years ago, Cadence was able to talk Jackson down when he learned that Lester had molested Jackie. Lester having a gun, played a significant role in that. Jackson wouldn't be any good to his daughter if he were dead.

Jackie hopped out of the truck, dropping her ice cream cone.

"Let's go." Cadence turned Jackie's body away from the violence and ushered her in the house.

"Is daddy going to die?"

"Dear God, no," Cadence reassured, pulling Jackie to her bosom.

"How do you know?" she sniffled, pushing away from Cadence. "Mommy got in a fight with Lester, and he killed her—— what if he does the same thing to daddy?"

Jackie's logic was on point, and Cadence understood how she came to the conclusion.

"This is not the same thing," she said, cupping Jackie's

face. "Lester doesn't have a gun."

At least that's what Cadence assumed. If he had, she'd be dead.

"Your cousins are out there with daddy, and the police are on the way," she added, sitting on the edge of the couch, relieving some of the tension pulling on her stomach. "Can you do me a favor?"

Jackie nodded, blinking away the tears.

"Go to your bedroom and stay there. I'll let you know when it's alright to come down."

She didn't utter a single sound as her feet shuffled across the floor. Cadence stood at the bottom of the stairs until she heard the door close.

So much had happened throughout the course of the day. The last thing they needed was Jackie seeing something she shouldn't. Cadence was grateful that Jackie's bedroom windows faced the rear of the house.

Cadence called Knox's personal number as she headed back outside.

"Hello."

"Lester—— attacked—— me," Cadence said in broken intervals. "He hid in the trunk of my car and blindsided me when I got home."

"Are you hurt? Where is he? Did you call the police?"

"I'm fine," she lied, walking down the stairs. "His ass is being handed to him by——"

"And the police?" Knox asked. "Have they been called?"

She hesitated. "Not by me."

"Cadence. Call them. Now," he demanded. "I'm on my way."

"It's not like they're going to do anything," she remarked, enjoying the street justice a little too much.

"But you still need to report it to cover your own hide," Knox countered. "We can add carjacking and attempted abduction to Lester's long list of charges, and say his injuries were a result of self-defense," he explained. "If you don't, it'll look like some vigilante shit."

"Okay," Cadence agreed before disconnecting the call.

She moved in closer. Lester laid in a heap; his face barely recognizable.

"I don't know where you guys came from," Cadence said, giving Jackson a side-eye. "But I'm glad you showed up when you did."

"That's what family does," Tony shot back, giving Jackson some dap. "We always got you."

"Let me return the favor," she said, ushering them to come even closer. "I have to report this, so I need y'all to get out of here," Cadence warned, unlocking her phone, and scowling at Lester.

"You don't have to worry about him going anywhere," Sly sneered, giving Cadence pause. "He couldn't walk, run, hop, or skip away if he tried."

"And don't worry about us," Tony added, cracking his knuckles. "I already called the cops. This asshole ain't the only one who has *connections* in the police department."

Chapter 15

"Why don't you go inside?" Jackson advised as the police sirens got closer. "I'll tell them what happened."

"They're going to want to talk to me; besides, I need to see them cuff and put Lester in the back of the squad car."

"Alright, tough girl," Jackson whispered, standing next to Cadence, hoping the close proximity would offer her some comfort while keeping a watchful eye on Lester, who laid in the street immobile.

He knew Cadence was terrified, but she'd never admit it. Jackson was grateful he had the foresight to have Sly and Tony on standby. *The first mind is always golden.*

Red and blue lights swarmed the block from both ends, boxing Lester in the middle of the street. The headlights dropped a spotlight on him as if he were the main attraction on center stage. Lester's hands moved to shield his eyes. Cops sprang from their vehicles with guns drawn.

"Hands in the air," ordered a hard-body, plain clothes, male officer wearing a skullcap, strategically moving forward.

Jackson scooped Cadence behind him, stepping backward.

"Do you have any weapons on you?" he asked, but Lester didn't answer.

A short female officer in a bulletproof vest moved in from the opposite direction and nudged Lester's leg with her foot. "I know you hear him talking to you."

"No," Lester mumbled, holding his trembling arms in the air.

"I better not find anything when I search you," she warned, rolling his bruised body over while the first officer came in closer with a gun aimed at Lester's head.

Jackson took in the damage they inflicted on the left side of Lester's face while the officer snatched his arms behind his back and cuffed him. His lips were split and bloody, his eye was swollen and sealed shut, and his nose had a gangster lean.

No part of Jackson felt guilty. Lester had no business coming after his wife. Period.

"I'm Officer Douglas," the plainclothes cop introduced himself to Jackson and Cadence. "Can you tell me what happened here?"

Cadence came from behind Jackson and eyed Officer

Douglas for an unnaturally long time, making Jackson think something was wrong.

"You're safe now," Jackson reminded her, concerned about Cadence's well-being. "Tell him what happened before I arrived."

Her eyes narrowed as she continued to stare at the cop as if she was searching for something.

"Take your time," Officer Douglas encouraged with a slight nod.

"We can do this in the morning if you're not up to it," Jackson suggested, turning to face her. "Whatever's most comfortable for you," he said, then turned to the officer. "If that's alright."

"Certainly."

"That won't be necessary," she responded, explaining everything truthfully, up until the part when Sly and Tony arrived on the scene. She told him Jackson pulled Lester off of her.

Jackson picked up where she left off, continuing with the abbreviated version of what happened to Lester thereafter. He didn't want to implicate Sly or Tony in any way.

"Wait a minute," Cadence whispered, balancing her weight on one foot. "Aren't you the cop who questioned me the night Braelyn was murdered?"

I'll be damned. Jackson surveilled the officer who appeared to be in his early thirties. He looked more seasoned than he remembered, but that could be from the stress of the job or the five o'clock shadow that darkened his lower cheek and chin, which was a serious infraction.

Police officers weren't allowed to have stubble or facial hair unless they had some sort of written approval issued from the Bureau Chief's Exemption from the Chicago Police Department's Clean-Shaven Policy Card.

He learned that searching police policy on google. If ever he or Cadence were in a situation with the police, Jackson would be knowledgeable of their rights, as well as anything that he could use against the cops. He didn't use to be so jaded, but after what happened …

Maybe Officer Douglas got a promotion.

"Yes. I was first on the scene that day," he answered, snapping his fingers and pointing to Cadence's car. Another officer rushed over, pulling on gloves before touching the trunk. "I'm so glad Officer Johnson called. We can finally file charges against Lester and make them stick and give your family closure."

"Officer Johnson," Jackson repeated, trying to hide the shock in his speech and expression.

He couldn't have been referring to his cousins, Sylvester and Anthony Johnson, right? When did that happen? And if they, or one of them, were a cop, why wouldn't they tell me?

"I knew it," Cadence mumbled under her breath, grabbing Jackson's hand. The exposed flesh on his knuckles stung from the pressure.

"This won't be like last time," Officer Douglas promised. "Lester evaded capture, but now, we got him, and a ton of evidence to guarantee he won't see daylight outside of the prison yard."

Cadence sighed. "That sounds good, but I won't be satisfied until he's sentenced."

Officer Douglas spun on his heels, aiming his gun, causing Jackson to grab Cadence abruptly, almost knocking her down.

Jackson scanned the area, following the direction of the gun.

"Stop where you are," Officer Douglas ordered, taking deliberate steps onto the sidewalk, leaving them partially shielded behind the trunk of Cadence's car.

Every cop on the scene had their weapons drawn in the same direction.

"ADA Aaron Knox," the man called out in a calm but loud voice. "Don't shoot. My credentials are in my inside breasts pocket on the left."

"Why is the ADA here?" Officer Douglas said to no one in particular.

"I was wondering the same thing," Jackson whispered to Cadence.

She tugged on Jackson's arm, and he bent over, bringing his ear to her mouth. "I forgot to tell you he was coming."

Douglas told an officer via two-way radio to verify Knox's credentials. Once confirmed, he ordered everyone to lower their weapons, then Knox proceeded in his direction.

"Good evening, Officer???" Knox raised an eyebrow.

"Kent Douglas, sir." They shook hands. "It's a pleasure to meet you."

"Where is he?"

"In the back of the squad," Officer Douglas replied.

"Jackson. Cadence." Knox walked over to them. "Are you alright?"

"Better now that Lester's in custody," Jackson replied, putting an arm around Cadence, catching movement in the living room blinds.

Jackie. How much had she seen or heard?

"Hang in there. We've got five days until the trial," Knox said with a slight turn of the corner of his lip. "And now we've got Lester."

"There's something I need to ask you," Cadence said to Knox.

"Not here," he warned.

"Jackie's downstairs," Jackson informed Cadence.

"Officer Douglas," she called out. "Are we done? My daughter needs me."

"Yes. I'll let your husband know if there's anything else we need."

Jackson watched as Cadence made her way up the front steps and into the house.

"Do you know how much longer this is going to take?" Jackson asked.

"He should be done extracting fingerprints and fibers from the trunk and backseat of Cadence's car soon," Officer Douglas said, glancing over at Officer Byrd pulling the chip and candy wrappers from the trunk and placing them in separate clear evidence bags. "I'll be escorting Lester to the county jail myself."

"If it's all the same to you," Knox interrupted, plucking keys from his pants pocket and clutching them in his fist. "I'll be tailing you to lock-up. This is not up for debate."

Chapter 16

"How is she?" Jackson asked, rushing into the living room, tripping over his feet.

"Shaken up, but okay," Cadence responded, touching his arms, which stabilized him. "Jackie had a lot of questions, and I answered them as best as I could, but she's asking for you."

"I can't go up there like this," he retorted, glancing down at his dirty clothes smudged with splotches of Lester's blood. "My hands—— they look rough like a street fighter. I don't want to scare her."

"You could never," Cadence said, lifting his hands and

examining the bruises. "Go shower. I'll toss these clothes in the washer, and when you're done, I'll put some ointment on your knuckles."

"I don't want Jackie to think I'm avoiding her."

"She just got out of the shower about five minutes before you came inside," Cadence countered, unbuckling Jackson's jeans. "She should be getting dressed for bed. I'll let her know you'll come upstairs once you're cleaned up."

"Thanks, baby," Jackson said, kicking off his shoes, stepping out of his jeans and boxers, then pulling the shirt over his head.

Jackson dug in his pants pocket, retrieving his wallet and phone before handing the clothing to Cadence. He placed the wallet on the side table but kept his phone.

Entering the bathroom designed with a Japanese theme, Jackson sat on the white bath bench encased in a block of glass from the floor to the ceiling. He dialed Sly's number, then Tony's. Both went straight to voicemail.

"Officer Johnson." Jackson grimaced. "Officer Douglas had to be mistaken."

After trying to reach his cousins a second time, he called their mother, Aunt Mable.

She was the matriarch of the family at seventy-five years young. No one thought she would have children, but at the age of forty-five, she gave birth to Sly and Tony, who were more like Jackson's little brothers than cousins when they were coming up. Jackson's grandmother passed when his mother was a teenager. Aunt Mable embraced the role of mother and raised her two siblings, putting them through college and making sure they never went hungry. Jackson would always treat her with the utmost respect.

"Hi, Aunt Mable."

"Jax, darling, is that you?" she asked, her voice shaky and tired.

"Yes, ma'am," he replied, wincing as he stretched his fingers. "I'm sorry for calling this late. I didn't mean to wake you."

"It's no bother, nephew," she replied, clearing her throat. "Anytime you call is a good time." Jackson could hear the smile in her voice. "What's troubling you?"

"I'm trying to get a hold of Sly and Tony, but neither of them are answering the phone. Have you heard from them?"

"They're at work," Aunt Mable replied, yawning. "You know they can't bring their phones in that jail."

"Ma'am?" Jackson's shoulders straightened.

"They have to keep them in the car. It's a liability or something like that; Sly tried explaining it to me," she said, yawning a second time. "But it never made sense. If I had an emergency, I'd have to call the prison, and someone would connect me. Hell, by the time they finally get him on the line, I'd be dead," she fussed, having a coughing fit.

"Are you alright?"

"Just a little cold stuck in my throat. Nothing a warm glass of water can't fix," Aunt Mable dismissed. "As I was saying—— I think it's a crappy system if you ask me."

"I agree," Jackson said, not wanting to go against her

beliefs, although he understood why the policy was in place.

"Did you want me to deliver a message for you?"

"That's alright," he countered. "Do you know what time they get off?"

"Six," Aunt Mable answered. "But they don't make it home until seven thirty-ish."

"Thanks, Auntie. I appreciate it. Now go back to sleep."

"Anything for my favorite nephew," she shot back. "And don't let another four years go by before I see you again."

"Yes, ma'am."

Jackson ended the call and placed the phone inside a waterproof compartment in the wall.

Sly and Tony. Correctional officers. "Wow," he mumbled, pressing a platinum panel.

A large mirrored square in the ceiling illuminated, and a hot downpour of water massaged the top of his head and tense shoulders.

Jackson emerged from the bathroom, feeling refreshed with Lester's smut washed down the drain. He tucked the bath towel around his waist, sat on the side of the bed, and laid back.

"She's finally down," Cadence said, entering their bedroom, claiming the space next to Jackson, and lying back.

They looked like two people relaxing on a beach towel, sunbathing, staring at the clear blue sky. Cadence turned into him, resting a hand on his chest. The warmth of her touch was comforting.

"Thanks," Jackson said, angling his body toward Cadence, pulling her even closer. "I didn't want her to see me like that."

"I know."

He closed his eyes, laying his face against her soft hair. "I called Aunt Mable, and she told me the twins work at Cook County Jail. Whatcha think about that?"

"Wowwwwww."

"That's exactly what I said," Jackson shot back.

"They have the grit for it. That's for sure," Cadence commented, propping on her elbow, forcing Jackson to adjust his angle. "I take it their presence tonight wasn't by coincidence."

He propped on his elbow and gazed into her eyes. "After that first night back, I couldn't take any chances. I know I should've told you, but I didn't want to argue," he said, placing a finger over her lips when she started to protest. "Superwoman needs extra protection sometimes, too."

"Thank you." Cadence smiled, pursing her lips against his finger. "I appreciate you."

* * *

A bone-curdling screech woke Cadence and Jackson from their sleep.

"Jackie," he shouted, kicking off the covers and climbing out of bed half-awake.

He knocked over the table lamp, dashing across the room.

"Jackson. Wait," Cadence yelled, digging in the drawer and tossing him a pair of boxer shorts.

He tripped over his feet while stepping into the boxers,

then took off running toward the stairs with Cadence on his heels.

"Daddy," she shrieked as Jackson barged into her bedroom, turning on the light.

She was huddled in a fetal position on the bed with her back against the wall.

"Daddy's here, baby," Jackson said, sitting on the bed. It was damp.

Jackie climbed into his arms, weeping. He looked up at Cadence, and she seemed troubled and concerned; all the things he was feeling.

"Did you have a bad dream?" he asked, holding her tight.

She cried even harder.

"You can tell us," Jackson said, rubbing her back. "We're here to make everything okay."

"But you can't," Jackie mumbled, pushing away from him. "Don't promise to do something that's impossible."

Cadence sat beside them. "What do you mean, darling?"

"Ms. Donnella said she can't promise to make things better. How can you promise to do that if you don't even know what's wrong?"

He glanced at Cadence.

Jackie had a point. Her therapist, Ms. Donnella, had been working with her since they moved to Stuttgart. It took some time, but she had pulled Jackie out of her shell and gave them their happy daughter back.

"Did you have a nightmare about what happened tonight?" Jackson asked.

Jackie's grip around his middle got tighter, and she buried her head further into his chest. Her hair shielded her face from view.

He and Cadence shared a worried glance.

"Lester can't hurt you or me," Cadence reassured Jackie. "He's been arrested."

She slowly lifted her head, wiping the tears away. "In my dream, he killed you and daddy, then told me I was going to be an orphan. When I tried to fight him." Jackie began to cry again. "He vanished, and I was in an abandoned building with hundreds of girls in raggedy clothes. We didn't have any food or water, and no adults were there to take care of us."

"That's horrible," Jackson remarked, rocking her. "No wonder you woke up screaming."

Cadence scooted closer. "I'm sorry that Lester came back into our lives, but he is in custody and will be for a long time."

"But it seemed so real, especially after he got in that fight with daddy."

"Nightmares can feel very real, but I can assure you that your daddy and I will never let him hurt you."

Jackie looked up at Jackson with questioning eyes. "Daddy. Is that true?"

"That's a promise," Jackson vowed, cupping her face and placing a kiss on her forehead.

"Can I sleep with y'all tonight?"

"Sure thing," Jackson said, and the three of them embraced.

Chapter 17

The following morning, Jackson woke Jackie up just in time for her to sign-in for her virtual learning class through Zoom. It started at seven-thirty in the morning, which translated to one-thirty in the afternoon in Stuttgart.

He and Cadence discussed enrolling Jackie in her previous school in Chicago for the remainder of the term, but since it was already late January and Jackie's grades were exceptional, they agreed to let her finish up the school year via e-learning with her school in Stuttgart.

"Good morning, Jackie," Jackson said, smiling, wiggling her toes. "Time to get up, sleepyhead."

Jackson was on the fence about making her sign-on today after the rough night she had, but he wanted to keep her routine normal, and not give much weight to the Lester incident. Although, he and Cadence would keep a close eye on her to make sure she's okay.

"Ms. Schneider's waiting for you," he warned, pulling the covers back. "If you're not logged in by the time she takes attendance, you'll be marked absent."

"I knowwwwww," Jackie grunted, reaching for the covers. "Five more minutes."

"It's seven-twenty-three," Cadence called out from the dining room. "Let's get it. Your breakfast and hot cocoa are on the table."

"You better hurry up before I eat your food," Jackson teased, walking toward the door. "A second helping of chocolate chip pancakes, scrambled eggs, and bacon would hit the spot."

"Daddy quit playing," Jackie whined, sitting upright and stretching her arms.

Jackson turned, examining her face. Jackie's eyes were a little puffy, but other than that, she looked normal. He knew that didn't mean Jackie was okay, but at least, it wouldn't trigger any questions from Ms. Schneider. She'd probably think Jackie didn't get enough sleep, and she would be right.

Once Jackie got settled into her class, Jackson went to the media room to call Sly. He got comfortable on the leather recliner, put his feet up, and stared at the blank seventy-inch flat screen.

"Hey man, is there something you want to tell me?" Jackson asked, rotating the remote in his hand.

"First things first, cousin. I didn't know you could still scrap like that. It's nice to see you haven't lost your fighting abilities," Sly commented; a sense of pride dripped from his voice. "You missed your calling. We could use a guard like you, Jax. Someone that can hold his own, who's not afraid of getting physical with these knuckleheads."

"And that brings me to why I called," Jackson commented, tossing the remote on the recliner beside him. "When did you become a corrections officer?"

"It's going on three years now," Sly responded. "Tony talked me into it. He was already in the training program and convinced me to join."

"Doesn't your record have to be clean?"

"My record *is* clean," Sly fired back. "I'll be the first to admit, I did some dumb shit when I was younger, and some stuff that should have me under the jail, but I wasn't stupid enough to get caught. Thank God and my momma for sparing Tony and me."

"Why didn't you mention it?"

"You never asked," Sly replied. "Besides, the hood doesn't know what we do for a living. We dress at work and change before we leave. If the bangers knew we were correctional officers, my information train would dry up. I hear about all kinds of things."

"I bet you do."

"Anyway. I was at work when transport brought Lester in," Sly stated with a devilish snicker. "He didn't look too good."

"You don't say," Jackson remarked, and they shared a hearty laugh.

As they simmered down, Sly added, "I didn't see him much. They probably took him to the infirmary."

"Do you think Lester recognized you?"

"I'm positive he did," Sly confirmed, sounding very sure of himself. "This isn't his first stint in the joint. He knows how it works. He ain't no snitch."

* * *

Soon as Jackson was done speaking with Sly, he reached out to Ms. Donnella and explained what the last three weeks had been like for Jackie, focusing on last night's confrontation and the nightmare. He wasn't sure how to help his daughter, but he knew Ms. Donnella was the best place to start. She agreed to work Jackie into her evening schedule at seven o'clock, which was perfect. That was noon Chicago time, giving Jackie a chance to finish her virtual classroom sessions and have lunch.

The rest of the afternoon went by without incident. They visited Caden, ordered a pizza to be delivered by the time they returned home, and was able to watch The Secret Life of Pets with Jackie before she went to bed.

Cadence turned in early. He straightened up the house and made sure it was cleaned to her liking, leaving her nothing to do when she got up in the morning. Jackson had finally settled in the bed when his phone vibrated. He almost didn't answer because he didn't recognize the number.

"Hello."

"Jax. He's gone," Sly said, panting like he was in the throes of an asthma attack. "I don't know where the hell he is."

"Who?" Jackson asked with bated breath, fearing Sly's response.

"Lester," he whispered into the phone. "I don't know who he knows to pull these kinds of strings, but he isn't here."

"How's that possible?" Jackson spoke in a hushed tone. "He has warrants."

"I don't know," Sly said, his voice lower than before. "I checked the infirmary. He's not there. Maybe he got transferred to another facility or something. But the bottom line is, Lester isn't here. I wanted to give you a heads up. I gotta go."

Not even a full twenty-four hours had passed, and Jackson's promise to his baby girl guaranteeing her safety from Lester had been voided. His rap sheet was way too extensive for him to be out on bond. As far as Jackson knew, Lester hadn't even gone before a judge for arraignment. If a person had warrants against them, do they still get to be arraigned?

Jackson glanced over at his wife, who was sound asleep. He hated to do it, but he had no choice. "Cadence, wake up," he said, nudging her arm. "Baby, wake up."

She rolled over, snuggling the pillow.

"Cadence." Jackson shook her hip.

"You still can't have none," she said mid-snore.

He shook his head, then tried again.

"What is it?" She stirred, glancing around. "Did Jackie

have another bad dream?"

"No." He sighed. "Just go back to sleep. We'll talk in——"

She was snoring before he could finish his sentence.

Chapter 18

Cadence awakened to the aroma of freshly brewed hazelnut coffee permeating the air.

"Mmmmm, that smells so good," she purred, entering the kitchen.

Jackson already had a cup waiting for her.

"Thank you." Her nose hovered above the rim before taking a sip. "I slept so good last night."

"I know. I tried to wake you."

"Now, baby. You know all my good stuff is off-limits for another three weeks," Cadence teased, doing a little sexy dance in a black gown that stopped several inches above the knee.

"Funny," Jackson smirked. "You told me the same thing when I tried to wake you, but you don't remember anything else."

"Well, that's usually what you're aiming for when you disturb my slumber in the middle of the night."

That's true.

"Last night was the exception," Jackson countered, pulling out a chair for her to sit.

"Thanks," she said, staring at her husband, analyzing his mood. Jackson didn't seem like himself. "Why you look like you lost your best friend?"

He claimed the seat beside her, removing the coffee mug from her hands. "Lester's not in jail."

"What?" Cadence bounded from the seat, almost knocking over the chair.

Jackson grabbed her wrist, holding Cadence in place. Her pulse slammed into the palm of Jackson's hand.

"Sly called last night and told me that Lester isn't there. He thought Lester might be in the infirmary, but he wasn't there either."

"Why didn't you wake me?" She fussed, then remembered that he attempted to. Sitting back down, Cadence asked, "Can you tell me how that's even possible? He was arrested. We saw it with our own two eyes."

"I'm just as stunned as you are," Jackson replied, releasing her wrist.

"Why can't things go the way they're supposed to? Is that

too much to ask?" she said, taking the coffee from Jackson's hand and leaving the kitchen.

"Where are you going?" Jackson called out, following Cadence into the dining room.

"I need to call Knox. He should be able to tell us something."

"Especially since he escorted Lester to the county jail," he commented.

"Come again?" Cadence frowned, turning to face Jackson.

"Knox told Officer Douglas that he was following them there."

"What's really going on?" she remarked, sitting on the bed and dialing Knox.

"Good morning," Jackie dragged, rounding the corner, glancing into the bedroom before making her way to the dining room.

"Good morning, baby," Cadence replied, waving Jackson out of the room.

"Log on for class, and I'll fix you something to eat," Jackson said to Jackie, shutting the door behind him.

"May I speak with ADA Knox, please."

"I'm sorry this is the answering service. Mr. Knox will be in at nine, if you would like to call back at that time, the receptionist will be able to assist you," the woman said, sounding like she hit the power ball jackpot. "Would you like to leave a message?"

"No, thank you," Cadence replied, ending the call, then checked the time on her phone. It was seven in the morning. "What am I thinking?" she mumbled under her breath.

As tempting as it was, Cadence resisted the urge to call Knox on his cell at this hour. She emerged from the bedroom, took a quick shower, then joined the family for breakfast.

Cadence and Jackson cleared the morning dishes from the dining table as Jackie started her lesson with Ms. Schneider and the class.

"Mama Cee," Jackie called out, muting the laptop.

"Yeah."

"Can I go with you to visit Caden today?"

"Yes," she responded, grabbing the butter dish. "Now, focus on what you're supposed to be doing."

Jackie smiled, then turned her attention back to the screen.

Cadence entered the kitchen as Jackson was loading the dishwasher. "What did Knox say?"

"Nothing."

Jackson glanced at Cadence over his shoulder.

"My mind is so blown over this that I've lost my senses," Cadence said, opening the refrigerator. "It's not even eight o'clock in the morning."

"Damn." Jackson glanced at the illuminated display on the microwave. "I didn't realize how early it was."

"I don't know how much longer I can deal with this," Cadence admitted in a low voice. "The stress of it all is starting to get to me."

The doorbell chimed, sending Cadence jumping toward Jackson.

"See what I mean," she said, straightening her shirt. "This is what I'm talking about. My nerves are shot to shit."

Jackson caressed her cheek. He didn't utter a sound.

The doorbell chimed again.

"Mama Ceeeee," Jackie shouted.

"I got it," Cadence responded, leaving the kitchen, sweeping past Jackie, and into the living room. "Who is it?" she asked, pulling the sheer curtain to the side, peering out of the frosted oval glass.

"DCFS."

"Jackson," she yelled, holding onto the doorknob, but not unlocking the door.

"Who's that?" he asked, rushing in the living room, moving Cadence aside, and looking out of the glass. "Who is it?"

"Department of Children and Family Services," answered a woman with a tenor voice, deeper than his.

"Yes," he said, opening the door, but not the screen.

"We're looking for Jackson Goldsmith, parent of Jacqueline Nevels," the woman said, flashing an ID attached on a lanyard around her neck.

Cadence moved in closer, examining the name on the ID. The masculine voice belonged to, Glenda Powers. She glanced over at another woman, Bea Evers, with the same identification, and two male police officers who were built like they tied for first place in a body-building contest.

"May we help you?" Cadence asked, frowning.

Glenda ignored her, then glanced up at Jackson. "Are you Jackson Goldsmith?"

"Yes," he responded, opening the screen door.

"You're under arrest," said Bea, who was shorter in stature

and a thousand times more attractive than Glenda."

"Excuse me," Cadence interjected, standing beside her husband. "You don't have the authority to arrest him."

"But we do," a big, burly cop said, signaling his men, and they brushed past the DCFS representatives, grabbing Jackson.

"For what?" he asked, and the bass in his voice rumbled the walls.

That beating Jackson and the twins put on Lester has come back to haunt them. But why would DCFS be involved?

"What's wrong, daddy?" Jackie ran to the front.

"Wait a minute," Cadence shouted, trying to get between the cops and Jackson. "What are you arresting him for? What did he do?"

"Let my daddy go," Jackie shrieked.

Immediately, Cadence stopped tussling, and she scooped Jackie in her arms.

"Please tell me what you think I've done?" Jackson pleaded.

They pushed him against the wall so hard that the side of his face was smashed in. Jackson's right jaw disappeared into his mouth, which was forced open from the pressure.

"Do you have to handle him like that in front of his daughter?" Cadence asked, covering Jackie's eyes with her hand. "He's not resisting. Please, stop. He just wants to know why you're arresting him?"

"Truancy," Glenda stated, folding her arms across her petite breasts.

"What?" Jackson mumbled.

"Jackie's homeschooled," Cadence said, glaring at Glenda and Bea. "She has e-learning with her teacher every day. That's what she was doing when you barged into our home."

"There's no record of her going to school at all this term," Bea added.

"Didn't I just say she was homeschooled," Cadence snapped, and every nerve ending in her body was taut.

Jackie tore from Cadence's arms. Within seconds, she was back with her laptop showing them Ms. Schneider and her classmates in Stuttgart. "I was doing my math assignment. See. Look." Jackie shoved the laptop in Glenda's face.

"Well, that's not what our records show." Bea shrugged, talking to Cadence. "You need to straighten that out with the school district, but as of right now, Mr. Goldsmith has to come with us."

"Please, don't do this," Cadence begged, tears welling in her eyes.

"Don't take my daddy." Jackie dropped to her knees and pressed praying hands together. "Pretty pretty please, don't take my daddy."

"Jackie," Jackson called out as the officers cuffed, and yanked him off the wall. "Everything will be okay."

"This isn't right," Cadence shouted, pulling Jackie from the floor.

"This can go one of two ways," Glenda countered, standing with her legs spread apart. "Either we remove the child from the residence and place her in a foster home, or——"

"Noooooooo," Jackie squealed, running toward the back

of the house.

"*Or*, Mr. Goldsmith spends thirty days in jail while you figure this out," Glenda concluded. "The choice is yours."

Chapter 19

The frigid January wind had no effect on Cadence as she stared, transfixed in the doorway, clutching her midsection as the police carted Jackson off. Her breakfast performed tricks in her stomach, and it took everything she had not to retch where she stood.

The whole scene was a huge misunderstanding. True, Jackie wasn't on the school's file this term, but she hadn't been in the Chicago Public School's system since first grade. There was no reason why she should be flagged now unless a neighbor or someone close to them reported seeing Jackie home during school hours, but why would they do that? No one knew the circumstances of her being home. It didn't make sense.

She slammed and locked the door. "Jackie. Honey. Where are you?" Cadence moved through the house toward the enclosed sunroom where she saw Jackie run off to. As she passed through the dining room, Cadence lifted the laptop that was teetering on the edge of the table. "Jackie. Come out, please."

Cadence entered the kitchen just as Jackie emerged from the pantry on wobbly legs, holding

the phone to her ear.

"Who are you talking to?"

"Grandma," Jackie responded, her voice shaky. "She said nobody's going to take me away. Is that true?"

"Yes, baby," Cadence maneuvered around the kitchen table and swooped Jackie in a tight embrace. "You're safe here with me."

"What about daddy? We showed them people the laptop, but they still took him away."

"It's a misunderstanding that we're going to clear up," Cadence said, extending her hand. "Let me talk to grandma."

"What if they come back for me?" Jackie's lips trembled as she handed Cadence the phone.

"They aren't," she said, squatting in front of Jackie. "Go pack a bag with one week's worth of outfits and pajamas. You're gonna stay at grandma's house while I figure things out."

"I'm hiding at grandma's just in case they come back."

"More like you'll be in a place where I know you'll be safe until I find out what's going on and get your daddy back home," Cadence explained, touching Jackie's arm, giving it a reassuring squeeze. "Go get your things while I talk to grandma."

"Okay," she uttered, moving slower than a snail.

Cadence waited for Jackie to leave the kitchen and round the corner before she spoke. "Mama." She blew out an exasperated breath, standing and leaning her head against the pantry door frame. "I'm trying to keep my cool, but I'm freaking out. I don't know how much more of this I can take," Cadence exclaimed, picturing Jackson's face slammed against the wall for no reason. "The police arrested Jackson because Jackie hasn't been to school. DCFS wouldn't listen to reason, and they took him away like he was a criminal."

"Pull it together," Phylicia advised. "You can't fall apart. Jackie needs you to be on top of your game now more than ever."

"I know."

"You hurry up and bring that baby over here, and go handle your business," Phylicia said. "I don't know why you didn't call your sister while they were there. You know she works for DCFS."

"I forgot that Crystal's a social worker," Cadence replied, going to her bedroom, placing the phone on the dresser, and putting it on speaker. "She should be able to give me some information."

"That's what I was thinking. Crystal's been with the department for six years and should know the ins and outs," Phylicia added. "And call the police?"

"Why would I do that? They're the ones who arrested

Jackson in the first place."

"But a different set of cops may not know what's going on."

"I don't know about that. They've all been on dirt the entire time. I can't prove it, but I believe the police have had their hand in everything that's happened since we've been back."

Phylicia fell silent.

"I don't believe in conspiracy theories, but too many coincidences aren't coincidences at all."

"Exactly, mama," Cadence replied, brushing her hair back into a ponytail. "And it's wigging me out how Detective O'Brien isn't in custody awaiting this trial. He's out there free along with Lester." She paused at her new reality, and a shudder ravished her body. "And now I'm home alone, unprotected. Maybe that was their plan all along."

"You can always come stay with me."

"I'm not going to let them run me out of my home."

"Then I can come stay with you," Phylicia countered.

"Nah, mama. I want Jackie away from here for a few days, so she doesn't have a constant reminder of what's happened," Cadence explained, wrapping the ponytail holder around her thick hair. "But, thanks."

"I'm ready," Jackie said, standing in the doorway.

"Mama. We'll see you soon."

* * *

Within thirty minutes, Cadence pulled into her mother's driveway, parking behind a silver truck she didn't recognize.

"I wonder who's here," Jackie commented, lifting her bag from the floor and opening the door.

Cadence grabbed her wrist. "Wait."

"What did I do?" Jackie winced, trying to pull away. "You're hurting me."

"Shhhh," Cadence whispered, loosening her grip a bit, checking the rearview and side mirrors for anything or anyone out of place. "Close and lock the door."

Everything seemed to be in order, but she was still wary.

"Mama Cee, what's wrong?"

"Did grandma say she had company?" Cadence asked, dialing her mother's number.

"I don't remember."

"What's taking you so long?" Phylicia asked when she answered the phone. "Crystal's waiting on you."

Cadence released Jackie's wrist. "Does she drive a silver Pathfinder?"

"It's silver, but child, I don't know what kind of truck she has," Phylicia countered. "Are you outside?"

"We just pulled up."

"Well, get on in here. Crystal has to go to work," Phylicia shot back, then ended the call.

Cadence turned to Jackie. "I'm sorry for grabbing you like that. My nerves are all over the place and with everything that happened this morning——"

"It's okay, mommy."

Cadence's heart swelled. That's the first time Jackie had called her mommy, instead of Mama Cee. She'd slip up but always caught herself before the whole word came out. Cadence embraced her role as Jackie's stepmother and never once tried to replace or make her forget about Braelyn. She never knew how sweet the word sounded being directed at her. Cadence thought she'd have to wait until Caden was old enough to talk, and though this was probably a one-time occurrence, she reveled in the moment.

"Come on, baby," Cadence said as they climbed out of the car and headed toward the entrance.

Crystal stood in the doorway, looking even more beautiful than she remembered. Cadence smiled, taking in Crystal's glowing pecan skin, warm hickory eyes, and a figure that white men would call fat, but a brother would die and come back several lifetimes for. Crystal's golden-brown hair was curly and free-flowing around her face.

"Hey, Sissy," Crystal greeted, pulling Cadence into her arms. "God, I've missed you."

"I've missed you more," she replied, letting happy tears flow down her face, then pulling away. "This is my daughter, Jacqueline Nevels, but everybody calls her Jackie."

Jackie giggled, hip bumping Cadence.

"Nice to meet you, niece," Crystal said, opening her arms, and Jackie hugged her. "We're going to have so much fun."

"Where's my girl?" Phylicia called out from a distance.

"Go give grandma a hug before she gets jealous," Crystal teased, winking at Jackie.

"You're funny," Jackie commented, then ran off.

"She's adorable Cadence," Crystal said, closing the front

door and moving into the living room. They sat on the couch with their bodies angled toward one another. "What's this momma's telling me about Jackson being arrested and DCFS threatening to take Jackie?"

Cadence shared all the details of the ordeal with Crystal.

"I don't know what to do." Cadence shrugged, feeling defeated.

"This whole situation's terrible, and I'm sorry this has happened to you, especially that innocent child, but we're going to fight this," Crystal reassured, grabbing Cadence's hand. "First of all, they didn't follow proper procedure."

"What do you mean?"

"Did Glenda or Bea show you a warrant?"

"No." Cadence frowned. "Glenda asked if Jackson was Jackie's parent and, in the same breath, told him he was under arrest."

Crystal sighed, rolling her eyes. "They had no right to enter your home without a signed warrant from a judge unless you invited them in. You didn't have to open the door, but I'm sure they knew you wouldn't know that."

"Glenda forced us, saying that they would take Jackie and put her in foster care if Jackson refused to go with them."

"For truancy?" Crystal scowled, whipping out her phone. "That's some bullshit. The only reason the police would be with the social worker is if they believed the child was in imminent danger. Then and *only then*, they can enter your house without a warrant."

"Who would do this?" Cadence asked, flailing her arms.

"What's to gain by locking up my husband and trying to take my daughter away?"

"I don't know," Crystal replied, her thumbs sliding across the screen of her phone. "What were the worker's names again?"

"Glenda Powers and Bea Evers."

"I'll look into this when I get to the office," Crystal said, grabbing her coat off the arm of the couch. "The charges should be in Jackie's case file."

"Jackie doesn't have a file," Cadence retorted, staring at her sister. "She's never been in the system. Not even when she was with her mother."

"She does now since DCFS is involved," Crystal informed Cadence, sliding her arms in her coat, and lifting a black purse from the couch. "I'll be in touch. Love you, Sissy."

"Love you, too." Cadence embraced Crystal. "I need to call Jackson's parents, and let them know what happened. They're going to be devastated."

Chapter 20

As much as Jackson wanted to say something, he knew better than to question the police. His father drilled that into his brain as a young boy. The objective was always to be compliant, so he could live to see another day, which meant keeping his mouth shut, regardless of the injustice.

The officer guided Jackson by the head into the back of the unmarked police car. Residual marijuana fumes lingered in the confined space, burning his eyes and nose.

Glaring at Jackson, the officer slammed the door and sneered. He ignored the intimidation tactic and searched for a name or badge number on his uniform, but he had neither.

Jackson shifted on his hip, looking in the opposite direction for the second officer, but he was nowhere in sight.

Mere seconds past before Glenda and Bea occupied the front seats, catching Jackson off guard.

"Get comfortable," Glenda ordered, putting the butt of a blunt between her lips, lighting it, and taking a pull. "We got a long ride ahead of us. If you act right, I just might let you hit this." She smirked, blowing clouds of smoke through the gated partition in Jackson's face before pulling away from the curb.

"Stop fucking with him," Bea warned, loosening her ponytail, letting her shoulder-length hair fall, and placing a red and black checkerboard skullcap on her head. "We got enough shit to deal with without you antagonizing him."

Instantly, Steven's words played in his head. *Cops on Lester's payroll wear those hats.*

Bile rose from Jackson's stomach to the back of his throat. They had the perfect set-up, and the execution was flawless. What parent wouldn't do what was needed to protect their kid? The only thing he didn't understand was why.

"My daughter was never in danger of being taken from me, was she, *officer?*"

Glenda huffed, glancing over at Bea. "Took him long enough to figure it out."

The sarcasm in her heavy voice infuriated Jackson. He looked around, trying to figure out a way to escape, but he was at a disadvantage with his wrist cuffed behind his back. Jackson's heart raced as Glenda got on Interstate-57, heading southbound. He had no clue as to where they were taking him.

The burning question surfaced, and he couldn't help himself.

"How long have you been working for Lester?" he asked, but regretted doing so as soon as the words left his mouth. He knew better.

"You think you know something," Glenda spat, jerking the wheel to the far right, landing them on the shoulder with no guardrail.

Horns blared as traffic zipped by, recovering from the abrupt lane change.

Bea hopped out of the car and flung Jackson's door open. "You talk too damn much." Her fist crashed into his nose, causing it to bleed.

For a woman, she threw a solid punch. Jackson shook it off, never changing his expression. He refused to give Bea the satisfaction of knowing she hit like a trained boxer.

Glenda flipped the blue lights on atop the roof of the car, then snatched open the rear door on the driver's side. "You're determined to be a tough guy. Don't worry," Glenda said, holding up a syringe with a long needle.

"Get that the hell away from me," he barked, thrashing, trying to scoot away, but Bea was right there, blocking his movement.

"We're used to breaking cock-strong guys down like you," Glenda released a sinister laugh.

"I won't say anything else," Jackson pleaded as Bea straddled him and grabbed both sides of his head. "I'll do whatever you say."

"I know you will," Glenda remarked, plunging the syringe in his neck.

* * *

The doorbell rang, and Cadence dropped the glass she was washing in the sink. She ran full speed to the front door with Crystal on her heels. Her sister had been staying at the house since Jackson had been arrested.

Cadence pulled the curtain aside, then frowned. "Where have you been? I called you two days ago," she cried, swinging open the front door for Knox and another person. "Who's this?"

"Detective Xavier Carter," the burly dark-skinned man with perfect waves said, extending his hand, but Cadence didn't return the gesture. "I understand your hesitation considering everything you've been through. I'm going to find your husband, and that's a promise."

"I'm Crystal Edwards, her sister," she said, taking Cadence's hand and pulling her out of the entryway. "You're the one I spoke with over the phone."

"Yes, ma'am."

"Please, come in." Crystal moved aside, leading them to the sunroom.

"Knox, where is Jackson? Do you have any leads?" Cadence questioned. "I've called every precinct, and no one knows what I'm talking about. How is that possible? Where did they take my husband?"

"From here on," Detective Carter interjected, sitting on the edge of the tangerine cushioned sectional. "You speak directly with Knox or me."

"And how do I know I can trust you?" Cadence shot back. "It was two police officers that whisked him away."

"I vouch for him," Knox countered. "He's the one who's been running the covert investigation for me against Judge Duncan and Lester."

Cadence was distracted by Jackson's arrest that she forgot all about Lester, mysteriously missing from jail.

"We learned that Glenda Powers is actually Gloria Powell, and Bea Evers is Bernice Everly. Cops on Lester's payroll, and Glenda's his old girlfriend," Knox informed Cadence.

Crystal scooted closer to Cadence on the couch. "The DCFS angle was a roost."

"Why are you just now telling me this?" Cadence questioned Crystal. "I've been asking you for the past two days about those workers and you said you couldn't find any information."

"Don't be upset with her," Knox chimed in. "She was only doing what we asked. I didn't want her to say anything until we had more information."

"Well, what about the two guys that were with the women?" Cadence asked, glancing from Knox to Detective Carter. "Are they really cops?"

"No," Detective Carter replied. "They are enforcers in Lester's gang operation."

Cadence sprung to her feet. "What does that mean for my husband?"

"Does Lester have any beef with Jackson that you're aware of?" Detective Carter asked, staring into Cadence's eyes.

She fell silent, trying to decide if she should tell them about the fight the night Lester was arrested.

"Can you think of anything? No detail is too small," he added.

Cadence glanced at the detective, then said, "Lester attacked me several nights ago. He'd hid in the trunk of my car and ambushed me when I got home. Jackson was tailing me, but he made a detour." She swallowed, moving to the floor to ceiling windowpane. "I fought him off as best as I could." Cadence paused, remembering Lester's filthy hands on her body. "Jackson finally arrived and pulled Lester off of me."

"From the look of things, Jackson beat him pretty bad," Knox commented.

Detective Carter joined Cadence at the window. "This could be about revenge, or it could be about O'Brien's trial."

"Jackson doesn't have anything to do with that," Crystal said.

"But his wife does," Knox replied with his eyes fixed on Cadence. "This could be a tactic to throw you off before testifying or scare you from taking the stand."

"How do we know O'Brien isn't behind this whole thing?" Cadence asked, her voice trembling.

"We don't," Knox countered, leaning forward and resting his forearms on his knees. "I don't think he's stupid enough to come after you while his trial is pending."

"He'll just have someone else do his dirty work for him,"

Crystal growled, walking out of the room.

"I'll petition the court to see if we can have the trial pushed back due to the unusual circumstances," Knox said, getting to his feet.

"I hope so," Cadence muttered, keeping her tears at bay. "Because three days is too soon for me to take the stand and not know where my husband is, or if he's okay."

"That's what I'm afraid of," Knox said under his breath. "And that's what they're banking on."

Chapter 21

"Dear God, please bring my husband home to me, safe and unharmed. In Jesus' name, amen." Cadence made the sign of the cross, and then kissed her clutched fist as she rose from kneeling alongside of the bed.

She brushed the knees of her black slacks, pulled her hair into a neat bun, applied conservative makeup, then slipped on a pair of moderate heels.

"You ready?" Crystal asked, standing in the bedroom doorway.

"Not really, but what choice do I have?" Cadence responded, trying her best not to fall apart. "I can't do this without Jackson."

"You can," Crystal encouraged, moving closer and embracing Cadence. "I'll be right there the entire time. I know I'm not a substitute for Jackson, but use me. Pull your strength from me."

"I don't know what I would've done the past three days. You've been the biggest blessing. Especially, accompanying me to the hospital when I was afraid to go out alone. Because of you, I was able to maintain Caden's feeding schedule, giving him the nourishment he needs to keep his progress moving forward. He may be able to come home in a couple of weeks instead of months," Cadence expressed, trying to hold back the tears. "By then if not before, Jackson will be home, and this nightmare will be a faded memory."

"I'm here as long as you need me to be," Crystal reassured, squeezing Cadence tighter. "We're going to get through this, but right now, we have to get going. We don't want to get caught up in the rush hour traffic."

Cadence set the house alarm, then opened the front door. "Dear God," she screamed. "You almost gave me a heart attack."

"Detective Carter, what are you doing here?" Crystal asked, placing an arm on Cadence's shoulder.

"Good morning, ladies," he greeted, pressing praying hands together. "Please forgive me. I didn't mean to frighten you. I'm here to escort you to the courthouse."

"That's not necessary," Cadence countered, glancing at Detective Carter.

"Maybe not, but here I am anyway." He gestured toward

the stairs. "After you."

Cadence wouldn't admit it, but she was glad to see him.

"Any leads on finding Jackson?" Cadence asked, sliding into the backseat of the detective's car.

"We have some things in the works," he responded.

"What does that mean?" Crystal interjected, climbing in next to Cadence and closing the door. "You said something, but didn't give any information at all."

"You promised that you'd find my husband. I'm holding you to that Detective Carter. That's the only thing keeping me sane."

"And I will."

* * *

Forty-five minutes later, they pulled in front of the massive Cook County Criminal Court Building. Detective Carter parked, then walked the ladies inside and through security without incident. Instantly, Cadence flashed back to the first time she and Jackson came to court. Mayhem surrounded them. She'd give anything to go through that chaos again if it meant Jackson would be by her side.

The three of them entered the courtroom. Immediately, Cadence spotted Knox at the prosecution table bent over, looking at documents. She proceeded forward in his direction.

"Excuse me," a guard in a tan uniform said, grabbing her arm. "You can't go past the divider."

"Get your hands off of me," Cadence shouted, snatching away.

"Was that really necessary?" Detective Carter asked, stepping between Cadence and the sheriff. "You didn't have to handle her like that."

"What's going on here?" Knox asked, approaching fast.

"I was informing the lady that she needs to stay in the gallery," the guard replied.

Cadence cut her eyes at him. "I know that. If you look at where we are, it would be clear to you that I wasn't anywhere *near* the front of the courtroom."

"If you're going to argue with me, I will escort you off the premises."

"She's my witness," Knox defended, splaying a hand. "And she won't be going anywhere." He glanced at the guard's name badge. "Officer Grady, I'll take it from here."

Cadence gave him the evil eye as he tucked his tail and retreated to his station by the courtroom entrance.

"Are you alright?" Knox asked.

"I'm as fine as I can be under the circumstances," she replied, taking a deep breath. "Just antsy and missing my husband."

"We have a strong lead. I didn't want to say anything until everything was concrete," Knox commented, glancing at Detective Carter. "We're close to bringing him home. I just hate that it's taken this long."

"Thanks for everything that you're doing. Both of you," Cadence said, nodding at Knox and Detective Carter.

They all shared a glance and a smile, followed by a brief silence.

"You can't be in here during the proceedings," Knox warned, sliding his hands in the pockets of his black pin-striped slacks. "Judge Duncan said all witnesses must wait in the hall until called to testify."

"That wasn't a problem before," Cadence disputed, fidgeting with her wedding ring.

"If the judge is concerned about a witness changing his or her testimony based on what they heard while listening to the trial, he has a right to invoke such an order," Knox informed Cadence. "He has sole authority on that matter."

"Humph." Crystal huffed.

"Does this just apply to me, or are the other witnesses subjected to the same measures?"

"It's normal procedure," Detective Carter chimed in. "Usually, the police and sheriffs will provide security."

"The witnesses all wait together," Knox added, stepping in closer. "But if you're uncomfortable or just want to be alone with your thoughts until it's your turn to testify, you can wait in a separate room," he whispered, coming in even closer. "Truthfully, with everything going on, I prefer you to wait in an isolated area with trusted law enforcement." Knox angled a steely gaze on Detective Carter. "We can't be too careful."

"I'm on it," he responded. "We can sit in the hall up until the trial starts; that way, Crystal can be with you."

"Thanks." Cadence forced a smile.

People trickled inside the courtroom. They still had thirty

minutes until the trial started.

Cadence and Crystal claimed the bench to the left of the doors while Detective Carter stood guard.

"Hey Steven," Cadence said, bounding to her feet as he approached. "Thanks for coming to support me."

"Steven Bekker," a woman called out, wearing a cream pantsuit, cutting him off before he had a chance to speak.

"I'm sorry. I didn't have a choice." He mouthed to Cadence before giving the woman his attention. "Yes."

"Do you have your subpoena?"

Cadence eyed the professionally dressed woman. Her face was so stern and wrinkle-free that she resembled a plastic barbie doll.

"Yes," Steven responded, handing an envelope to the woman.

"Follow me," she instructed.

Steven glanced at Cadence and said, "Sorry."

Cadence watched as Steven trailed behind the woman like a trained animal.

"Who's that?" Crystal asked, glancing at Cadence.

"I don't know," she replied, continuing to watch them until they disappeared behind a door with a guard standing post.

"That's Maria Pious, co-counsel for the defense," Detective Carter said. "She's taking Steven to the holding area for their witnesses."

"Come again," Cadence shot back, tilting her head to the side.

"Steven is testifying for the defense."

Chapter 22

"Unbelievable," Cadence whispered, covering her mouth with the palm of her hand. "Why wouldn't he tell me?"

"I can't answer that," Detective Carter replied. "Steven must have testimony pertinent to their case; otherwise, they wouldn't be bothered."

"He's Braelyn's biological brother, and he did help her, and Lester try to steal money from me," Cadence said, noticing two women gaping at her as they walked in her direction with a sheriff escorting them. "I don't know how that would help Detective O'Brien's case."

"Any good lawyer has a way of twisting the truth or their

version of the truth to work in their client's favor," Detective Carter replied, giving a courteous smile to the passerby's. "Reed is the best defense attorney in the country. He isn't any different."

"Do you know them?" Crystal asked, nodding in the women's direction. "Because they are staring like they know you."

"I've never seen them before."

"That's Kenya Snell and Venus Dawkins," Detective Carter said, altering his stance. "They are the other witnesses testifying for the prosecution."

"No wonder," Cadence whispered, folding her hands in her lap. "Knox told me they only agreed to testify because I was." She sighed. "I'm curious as to what Detective O'Brien did to them."

"Courts about to start," a guard said, grabbing the handles of the doors.

Crystal stood. "You're going to do great," she reassured, kissing Cadence on the cheek, then hurried inside.

"This is it," Cadence mumbled, trying to command her runaway heartbeat to slow down.

The past four years all came down to this moment. Cadence closed her eyes and prayed that Detective O'Brien would be found guilty on the conspiracy to commit murder, that Jackie would get justice for the role he played in covering up the killing of her mother, that he would spend the rest of his life behind bars for witness tampering, and that she would finally be set free of her fears and could stop looking over her shoulder.

"Let's go," Detective Carter said, interrupting her prayer. "Our holding room is a few doors down the hall. Someone will come to get you when it's your turn to take the stand."

"Can we just sit here?" Cadence asked because she didn't trust her feet to carry her weight.

"Knox would prefer for you to stay out of sight until——"

"I know," she countered, searching his eyes. "But I have you, and I trust that you wouldn't let anything happen to me."

After a brief silence, Detective Carter glanced down at Cadence and said, "Okay." He placed his hands on the tactical belt around his waist, equipped with a service weapon, handcuffs, flashlight, and radio. "But if I get the wrong vibe … to the room we go."

In less than ten minutes, Venus rounded the corner in a pencil skirt, and a floral blouse with kinky-twist swirled in a pile on top of her head. She glanced at Cadence and gave a timid smile. Cadence nodded in response. She could feel Venus' nerves pipe through her body.

"Whewwww." She breathed out.

"You good?" Detective Carter asked, claiming the spot next to her.

"Yea."

"It's natural to feel nervous."

Cadence swallowed. "Am I next?"

"I'm not sure of the order."

Fifteen minutes later, the courtroom doors flew open, and Venus hightailed it out of there. Mascara ran down her face.

Cadence jumped up and reached for Venus.

"Hey. What're you doing?" Detective Carter asked, grabbing Cadence by the arm. "You can't talk to her."

"Huh?" Cadence turned and glared at him. "But, she's hurting."

"Cadence Goldsmith," a woman in a sheriff's uniform came from around the corner. "You're next. When the doors open, walk to the front of the courtroom and take the stand."

"Okay," she responded, and it felt like Cadence's chest cavity was caving in with every breath she took.

"I'll be right there in the back of the courtroom," Detective Carter said, touching her shoulder. "If you get nervous, look to me."

"Will do. I——"

Detective Carter lifted his arm in the air with a closed fist, and Cadence's speech halted. He stood, stepping in front of Cadence in a protective stance, gripping his service weapon.

"Hey," an agitated man's voice shouted. "I have some important information that I have to get——"

"That's Sly. My cousin," Cadence called out, sliding to the opposite side of the bench and standing.

"What the heck are you doing?" Detective Carter asked, half turning around.

"I'm looking for Xavier Carter," Sly shouted over the sheriff that was blocking him from entering the area outside of the courtroom.

"Detective Carter," the sheriff said, holding a hand in front of Sly. "He can speak with you once the witness enters the courtroom. No one can be in this area that isn't part of the case for security reasons."

"It's about Jackson," Sly said in a raised voice.

"Go see what he wants." Cadence pushed Detective Carter forward. "Maybe he knows where Jackson is."

The courtroom door opened.

Cadence's heart slammed against her ribcage, and the back of her throat tightened.

"Let's do this." Detective Carter nodded, gesturing for her to enter into the courtroom.

"No," she fired back, and her voice cracked. "Go get my husband."

"Come on," Sly bellowed, peering around the guard with wild eyes.

"Go on," Cadence urged, glancing back at the awaiting guard standing in the entryway.

"Ms. Goldsmith," the female sheriff said with a little more bass in her tone. Her agitation was evident.

Cadence glared at Detective Carter. "I'll be fine. Go."

He took off toward Sly. Cadence straightened her shoulders and entered the courtroom.

All eyes were on her as she approached the front. The only thing she could think about was Jackson. She crossed the infamous divider, then maneuvered around and stepped up onto the witness stand. The wooden box seemed even more massive than it does from the gallery.

The Court Clerk's heels clicked across the marble floor as she positioned herself in front of the witness stand, holding a bible in front of Cadence.

"Place your left hand on the Holy Bible and raise your right," she instructed. "Do you solemnly swear that you will tell the truth, the whole truth, and nothing but the truth, so help you, God?"

"I do."

"Please be seated," she said right before walking away.

The sea of blue uniforms on the defense's side of the courtroom took up all the space in Cadence's head. She refused to look at Detective O'Brien or his attorney.

"Good morning, Mrs. Goldsmith," ADA Knox greeted, buttoning his suit jacket as he came forward. "Why were you at Braelyn Nevel's house on the day in question?"

"Braelyn was leaving her boyfriend, Lester James. She and her daughter were moving in with me and my husband," Cadence explained, keeping her focus on Knox. "I went by to make sure she was okay."

"Were you concerned for her safety?"

"Yes."

"Why?"

"Because Lester beat her, and he molested her daughter."

The jurors gasped.

"Relevance." Reed stood, leaning forward on the table. "Who's on trial here? Why are we talking about a known drug dealer that has nothing to do with my client?"

"I'm establishing the timeline and how Mrs. Goldsmith came to be in contact with the defendant," Knox refuted, glancing at Judge Duncan.

"I'll allow it, but hurry up and make your point."

"Thank you, Your Honor," Knox said, then put his focus back on Cadence. "What did you discover when you went inside Braelyn's home?"

Cadence hated to relive that gruesome encounter all over again.

"Braelyn was lying on the floor in a pool of blood, clutching a gun," Cadence recalled, lowering her eyes. "I saw the back of a man running out the rear door."

"Is that man in the courtroom today?"

"Objection." Reed bounded from his seat. "Mrs. Goldsmith just said she didn't see the man's face."

"Mr. Knox," Judge Duncan said in an unsavory tone. "Stick to the matters of this case. This is your last warning."

Cadence didn't know why Knox asked her that question. She had told him a long time ago that Lester was the gunman. Braelyn had said his name while taking her last breath.

"What happened next?" Knox continued.

"I called the police, but by the time they arrived, Braelyn had passed away."

"Did the police question you?"

"Yes," Cadence proceeded, feeling anxious. "After they were done, Officer Douglas gave me a business card and told me to come to the station in the morning for more questioning."

"Then what happened?"

"I was getting ready to leave with my husband when Detective O'Brien approached us. He said he was with the Major Crimes Unit, and told me I needed to come with him to the Area South Police Station." She swallowed, trying to keep her breathing under control. "I told him Officer Douglas asked me to come in the morning. He told me that he had questions that couldn't wait until then. The whole time Detective O'Brien talked to me, he held a hand over his gun. I think he was trying to scare me."

"Speculation," Reed said, thrusting his hands forward. "How does she know my client's state of mind?"

"Stick to the facts, Mrs. Goldsmith," Judge Duncan ordered, peering at Cadence over the rim of his glasses. "Your opinion means nothing here."

His aura gave off a bad vibe. Cadence shouldn't feel that way about the judge—— O'Brien's attorney, yes, but not the judge.

Knox must have sensed her discomfort.

"Your Honor, may we request a short recess?" Knox asked. "Mrs. Goldsmith needs a moment to regroup."

Judge Duncan folded his hands in front of him. "I don't think that's necessary at this time. She seems perfectly capable of continuing," Judge Duncan said, glancing down at Cadence. "Proceed or rest so the defense can cross-examine."

Inadvertently, Cadence's eyes shifted to Detective O'Brien. The satisfying smirk on his face that followed the reprimanding she received from the judge spoke volumes. In her gut, she knew things weren't going to go her way.

Chapter 23

Cadence and Knox shared a glance, confirmation that she didn't imagine Judge Duncan's disdain for her.

Knox cleared his throat, then asked, "Did you go with Detective O'Brien?"

"Yes. I rode in the back of his truck to the police station," Cadence testified.

"Did anything unusual happen along the way?" Knox queried, standing an equal distance between the witness stand and the jurors.

"Yes. We were stopped at a traffic light down the street from Braelyn's house when Lester approached my window."

"Did you tell Detective O'Brien that Lester was alongside the truck?"

"No."

"Why not?"

"Because I was scared," she admitted. "Lester had the check I'd given to Braelyn in his hand." Cadence paused, glancing at the jury, then back to Knox. "The check had my home address on it. He knew where I lived. I couldn't do anything that might make him angry."

"That's understandable," Knox said, maneuvering into a spot that blocked Detective O'Brien from Cadence's view.

"What happened next?"

"He asked me why I was at Braelyn's house. Then he asked why I would give Braelyn a check and was I part of a drug deal that went bad. He said I had motive to kill her," Cadence explained, rubbing her hands along her thighs. "That's when I started secretly recording our conversation."

Knox walked to the prosecution table. "This recording right here," he said, lifting a clear plastic evidence bag with a flash drive inside.

"Objection," Reed shouted, almost knocking over the glass of water in front of him. "This evidence wasn't presented in discovery."

"It's the same evidence as before," Knox defended.

"How's that possible when you said all the evidence was destroyed during the break-in at your office," Reed countered, eyeing Knox with a loathing glare.

Cadence caught a glimpse from the corner of her eye of

Detective O'Brien. He wasn't looking as pleased with himself as he did when the judge scolded her.

"We discovered a back-up," Knox revealed, glancing at Cadence.

"How can we be sure of this recording's authenticity?" Reed asked, facing Judge Duncan.

"Your office received a copy this morning," Knox replied with a raised brow. "It's not my fault if your staff doesn't handle their affairs."

"That's enough," Judge Duncan ordered, glaring at both of them. "The evidence stays."

Cadence hadn't even realized that she was pinching the back of her hand. It didn't hurt until now. The entire case was built on that recording.

Knox inserted the flash drive into the laptop and cued the volume.

Whatever you think you know about what happened today, you better have fucking amnesia tomorrow when you speak with Officer Douglas. Do I make myself clear? Good. If you're feeling brave in the morning, just remember, I know where you live.

The jury, the folks in the gallery, and even Judge Duncan had stunned expressions on their faces.

"For the record," Knox said, closing the laptop. "Who's voice is that we just heard?"

"Detective O'Brien," Cadence responded.

"Where did this take place?"

"In the back of the police truck," she said, her voice

quivering. "Detective O'Brien threatened me while shoving his gun between my breasts."

"Speculation," Reed countered.

"Not if she's telling the events of what happened to her the way she remembers them," Knox argued.

"Overruled," Judge Duncan said, glancing at Cadence. "You may continue Mrs. Goldsmith."

"We arrived at the police station, but Detective O'Brien never took me inside. He pulled to the back of the parking lot beside a row of paddy wagons. I couldn't see anyone—— the truck was hidden from view," Cadence explained, gnawing her inner jaw. "Then, he pressed his gun into my forehead."

"What did you do?" Knox asked, stepping forward.

"Nothing." She shuddered, recalling the feel of the barrel on her skin. "I listened as he talked."

"What happened next?"

"Detective O'Brien slid the gun down the center of my face until it landed between my breasts. That's when he said, do I make myself clear. When I agreed, he got out of the car. I had been holding the phone between my knees. I quickly put it in my purse before he opened my door." Cadence paused, glancing at the jury who appeared to be hanging on her every word. "He then snatched me from the car. I screamed for help, but Detective O'Brien covered my mouth with his hand and told me to shut up before I make him do something I'd live to regret."

"Objection," Reed interjected, standing. "We didn't hear my client say that on the recording."

"Why wasn't that last part clear on the recording?" Knox questioned.

"My phone was in my purse at that point," Cadence stated, glaring at Reed. "If you listened closely, you can hear him. It's scratchy from moving around inside my bag with my things."

"Thank you for clarifying that, Mrs. Goldsmith," Knox said, stepping in front of Reed. "Please continue."

"Once I was compliant, Detective O'Brien told me to leave," she said, fidgeting with a gold stud earring in her earlobe, keeping her focus on Knox. "I ran to the nearest bus stop and went home."

"Thank you for your testimony," Knox said, moving behind the table, unbuttoned his suit jacket, and claimed his seat. "The prosecution rests."

"Cross, Mr. Reed." Judge Duncan angled a glance at the defense attorney.

"Hello, Mrs. Goldsmith," he greeted; his brown suit jacket was already unbuttoned since the last time he hopped up to object.

Reed moved from behind the defense table, and Cadence got a good look at him. She could tell he had an athletic build from the way the upper part of the suit jacket hugged his biceps. The closer Reed got to the witness stand, she could smell the musk aftershave or cologne on his golden-bronze skin. He was quite handsome, but that appeal didn't keep him from being a jerk.

"If you were as frightened as you say," Reed commented, leaning on the witness stand. "Why didn't you seek help?

You were right there at the police station. Why didn't you go inside?"

"Because I was afraid."

"You were afraid of my client?" he prodded.

"Yes."

"So why not speak to his superior?" Reed asked, propping on his elbow, invading her personal space. "Surely, you aren't frightened of all policemen."

Cadence sat back as far as she could. "Detective O'Brien had just told me——"

"Yes or no, Mrs. Goldsmith," Reed interjected, glaring at Cadence. "Are you frightened of all policemen?

"No," she responded, her voice trembling. "I didn't know what——"

"So, you made a conscious decision *not* to say anything to the people who could help you."

"Yes."

She glanced over at the rows of blue uniforms in the gallery behind the defense table. Every last one of the officers seemed annoyed by her presence. Some of them had to know what kind of cop Detective O'Brien was. Why would she trust any of them?

"Interesting," Reed commented, pacing in front of the witness stand.

Cadence was furious at the way Reed tried to twist her words, but she had to remain calm, or else he'd try to say she was irrational. Knox warned her about that.

The one thing that worked to her advantage was the

recording. No matter how Reed attempted to make it look like Cadence misinterpreted Detective O'Brien's actions while riding in the police truck, his own words caused the most damage.

"Excuse me, Your Honor," the bailiff said, rushing over to the bench.

Judge Duncan raised his hand, halting Reed's cross-examination. Cadence was thankful for the interruption. She needed time to regroup. Judge Duncan placed his hand over the microphone and pushed it forward.

Even though Cadence was sitting the closest to the judge, she couldn't make out anything the bailiff said to him.

After a few seconds, Judge Duncan removed his glasses and faced the jury. "You are excused," he said, gathering his things. "Court's adjourned. We'll reconvene tomorrow at nine."

Chatter filled the gallery. Cadence glanced at Knox as he sat with a perplexed expression.

Judge Duncan had disappeared into his chambers before Cadence stepped down from the witness stand.

Knox placed his MacBook Air and files in a leather briefcase, then met Cadence in the center aisle. "This gives us time to talk about your testimony."

"Not now," she said, brushing him off. "I have to see if they found Jackson."

Chapter 24

Jackson slipped in and out of consciousness. The air smelled of mold, mildew, and urine. His lips were sealed shut from lack of moisture, and his mouth felt dryer than crumbly chocolate cake. The cold penetrated the balls of his bare feet, and his toes were numb. He was too weak to open his eyes, but all of his other senses were on high alert.

"We've been here for three days. How much longer do we have to babysit?" Jackson heard Glenda's rough voice ask. "Can't we just kill him already?"

"After today, you can have your way with him," a male voice replied. "We'll dump his body on his wife's doorstep. That'll teach her ass to eff with me."

"Lester. What's one more day gonna do?" Glenda asked, grabbing Jackson's face, jerking it back and forth.

Jackson practiced staying limp, but it was hard not to flinch when she touched him. He hoped Glenda hadn't noticed.

"I promised Uncle Clark that no harm would come to him before O'Brien's trial, and I must keep my word. By the time we burn his ass alive, Uncle Clark will have me back in lock-up, eliminating me as a suspect. That's why."

Uncle Clark?

"Do you think Cadence is still going to testify?" Glenda asked, letting go of Jackson's face.

"I got word that she's at the courthouse," Lester replied. "My theory's that she'll be so messed up that O'Brien's attorney will rip her to shreds on the stand, making her look emotional and hostile."

"All I know is, O'Brien and the judge better hold up their end of the deal," Glenda growled. "I ain't going down for this shit. We did them a solid, and I expect immunity in return."

"Are you threatening my uncle?" Lester roared, his voice getting closer.

"I'm just saying; *you* have family loyalty. Judge Duncan doesn't owe me shit. How do I know he won't leave me hanging?"

Judge Duncan is Lester's uncle.

"Because he said he wouldn't, and that's all the confirmation you need," Lester shot back, his tone fiery. "Plus, if he did, he'd leave himself opened up for questioning. Uncle Clark has too much to lose. He's not about to put his livelihood on the line just to burn you, trust that if you don't trust anything else."

"Alright," she said, and Jackson could feel her standing close to him. "Let's get something to eat. It's not like he's going anywhere."

"How much of a dose did you give him?" Lester asked; his corn chip breath pricked Jackson's nose hairs.

It took everything in Jackson's power not to wince or sneeze.

"I'm surprised he's still out," Lester commented. "I just knew he was on steroids from the build of his muscular frame, but maybe not. Virgin lungs are more susceptible to sedatives."

"I can give him another dose," Glenda said, and every nerve in Jackson's body jolted.

"He's good, and even if he does come to, he ain't going nowhere." Lester released a mad man's laugh. "Let's go."

Jackson freed a breath he'd been holding. The further away Lester and Glenda's steps got, the heavier he inhaled and exhaled. Jackson forced his eyes open, and they felt like ten-pound barbells were sitting on each lid. He looked around. The room was dark with a glimmer of light coming through a tiny blocked-glass window. Concrete and steel beams were the only architecture in the place.

"This must be an abandoned warehouse or storage facility, but where?" he whispered as if someone would overhear him.

He tried to move his arms and legs, but they were bound to a metal chair with heavy rope.

All he could think about was getting home to Cadence and Jackie ... alive.

"Somebody help me," Jackson screamed; his raspy voice echoed off the hollow walls. "Can anyone hear me?"

If only Jackson had his phone, he could beckon Siri to call the police. They would be able to ping his location through the find my iPhone app. Jackson wasn't sure when his phone disappeared. The last thing he remembered was being in the back of the car with Glenda and Bea. He rotated his neck, and it was sore on the left side.

"Glenda drugged me," he uttered as the memory came rushing back.

Where did Bea go?

The only voices he'd heard off and on over the past three days were Lester and Glenda's.

"Heyyy," Jackson shouted, and this time his voice carried a little more as the saliva in his mouth replenished. "Can anyone hear me? I need help."

"Yea," a masculine voice barked back. "I can hear you *real* good."

"Lester," Jackson mumbled, kicking himself for not waiting long enough before he summoned for help.

"I told you I should've given him another shot," Glenda countered, digging in a backpack.

Lester circled Jackson. "I wonder what would've happened had I not forgotten my wallet."

"Not a damn thing," a third voice bellowed as heavy smoke filled the room.

Jackson's hearing sharpened, lasering in on the sound and direction of the voice. It came from the right.

"Show yourself before this becomes a bloodbath," Lester warned, grabbing Jackson by the back of the neck, and pushing a gun into the spot behind his ear. "I don't have a problem with killing him."

"You better be mindful what you say," a different voice cautioned, and Jackson recognized that one. It was his cousin, Sly. "Let him go, and you can walk out of here in one piece."

Jackson heard a click. The sound echoed in his ear from Lester, removing the safety from his gun.

"Don't do it," the first voice advised. "I already have your accomplice."

"Yeah, right," Lester egged the man on. "Ain't no way you came up on her that quick. She's police."

"So am I," the man shot back. "I trained this two-timing little shit. Taught her everything she knows. It's a shame that her talent has gone to waste."

"Xavier," Lester called out. "I know all about you."

"Is that right," Detective Carter replied.

"Shut up, Lester," Glenda ordered, sounding like she was the person in charge instead of him.

Jackson narrowed his eyes, but it was no help. He couldn't see anything through the smoke.

A gunshot hit the small blocked-glass window, shattering one of the squares. The wind whistled through the opening.

Lester knocked Jackson's chair over, then took off running. His footsteps didn't travel too far before a second gunshot blasted, resulting in Lester letting out a howling noise that resembled a wounded animal.

"Suspect down," Glenda called out, leaving Jackson more confused than ever.

"Jax, man. You good?" Sly rushed over as the smoke dissipated through the opening in the window. He pulled a utility knife from his pocket and cut the ropes. "Did that maniac hurt you?"

"I'm good," Jackson replied. "How's Cadence?"

"She's fine. Let me make sure you're alright," Sly commented, helping Jackson to his feet. "You have a nasty gash on the side of your head."

"I don't feel a thing," Jackson said, lifting a tingling arm to his temple. "My whole body feels numb."

Glenda came over with a heated blanket and wrapped it around Jackson. "The paramedics will start an IV, flushing your system with saline," she said, placing the chair upright and guiding Jackson to sit in it. "The side effects will wear off in a few hours."

"Who are you?" Jackson asked, glancing over at Lester.

Detective Carter had him in handcuffs, sitting on the floor with his back against the concrete wall. Lester's jean leg was covered in red from the knee to his ankle.

"My real name is Gloria, and Detective Carter is my handler."

Jackson absorbed that information, replaying everything from the DCFS arrest up until now.

"And Bea?" he asked as Sly took off his shoes and socks, and slid the warm knitted wool garments on Jackson's icy feet.

"She's in custody," Gloria replied.

"Is she really a cop?"

"Yep." Gloria nodded; her facial expression mimicked one of disgust. "She's as dirty as they come."

Jackson marveled at how Gloria and Bea played off of each other. He would never have thought that Gloria would be his saving grace. She was the cruelest of them all.

The paramedics rushed in, tending to both Jackson and Lester.

"How did you find me?" Jackson asked, looking beyond the female paramedic who cleaned the wound to his temple.

He knew there had to be more to the story since Sly was there.

"Not now. I'll tell you everything— later," Detective Carter said in a raised voice, cutting Sly off before he could explain. Then he placed his focus on Gloria. "Ride with Jackson to the hospital. Take him directly there. No stops."

"Yes, sir."

"Sly. You're coming with me," Detective Carter ordered, glaring at Lester. "We have unfinished business."

Chapter 25

Cadence made a beeline out of the courtroom and called Detective Carter. When he didn't answer, she called Sly.

"What's going on, Sissy?" Crystal asked. "Did they find Jackson?"

"I don't know," she shouted, stomping her foot. "Nobody's answering their phone."

"Come on," Crystal said, grabbing Cadence's wrist. "That guard looks like she's having a problem with us. Let's go to the lobby."

Cadence followed her sister to the elevators with her attention on the phone. She called them repeatedly, one after the other for ten minutes straight. Finally, Sly answered.

"Hey."

"Do you have Jackson?" she blurted out, making the guards in the lobby take notice.

"He's on his way to Mercy Hospital with Glenda. They may already be there. I mean—— Detective Gloria," Sly corrected. "But don't worry, Jax is okay."

"Gloria Powell. The dirty cop who pretended to work for DCFS," Cadence shot back.

"Sissy," Crystal said, touching Cadence's arm, but she shrugged her off. "This is neither the time nor the place to be talking foul about the police. We need to go."

"It's a long story, but trust me, she's one of the good guys," Sly reassured.

"Fuck that," Cadence bellowed in disbelief. "She barged into our house, threatened to put our daughter in foster care, and arrested my husband under false pretenses."

"Alright. Let's go." Crystal pushed Cadence toward the exit.

"What the hell are you doing?" Cadence barked, turning to face Crystal when she saw a group of Cook County sheriffs eyeing them ready to pounce.

Cadence did an about-face and left the building with Crystal by her side.

"Where are you?" Cadence asked Sly as she descended the concrete stairs, then paced along the sidewalk, side-stepping pedestrians.

"With Detective Carter," he replied. "I'll explain later."

"And you left Jackson with that woman."

"Trust me, Cadence. He's in good hands," Sly countered. "Tony's waiting for you at the hospital. I'll be there in a few."

"Sly," she called out, but he'd ended the call. "Ugh."

"What did he say?" Crystal asked, pulling the collar of her coat snug around her neck.

"Jackson's at Mercy Hospital."

"I'll get us an Uber."

Cadence forgot that Detective Carter drove them to the courthouse. The five minutes they waited for their ride seemed like an eternity. She couldn't wait to put her eyes on her husband. They climbed into the backseat, and the warmth of the car felt good. Cadence hadn't realized how cold she was. Her body was fueled by exhilaration and confusion as she tried to make sense of the information Sly divulged. Nothing he said was logical.

"Is Jackson alive?" Crystal leaned in and whispered.

"Yes."

"Is he hurt?"

"I don't know," Cadence responded, wringing her hands. "Sly says he's alright. The fact that he's alive is enough for me." She laid her head on Crystal's shoulder. "We'll worry about the rest as it comes."

Cadence closed her eyes, and they rode in silence for the duration of the trip.

The Uber driver pulled in front of the emergency room entrance. Cadence leaped out of the car before it came to a complete stop, and ran toward the automatic sliding glass doors.

"Where is he?" she asked Tony, who was posted against the wall looking like a model for a fashion outerwear magazine, wearing a black turtleneck, a lambskin leather bomber jacket, dark denim jeans, and lace-up Givenchy boots.

"Calm down," he said, clutching her arms. "Jackson's okay."

"Take me to him, please."

"Hey Crystal," Tony said, giving her a hug. "Y'all follow me."

They walked into the hospital and stopped at the information desk. The emergency room's waiting area was swamped with men, women, and children of all ages.

"We're here to see Jackson Goldsmith," Tony said to the woman in dark green scrubs behind the desk. "He's in room three."

"I'm sorry, but——"

Gloria walked over, stopped at the desk, and flashed her badge. "They're with me."

"Sorry, officer."

"Detective," Gloria corrected, then waved them forward. "This way."

Cadence huffed, glancing at Gloria as she fell in step with her. They moved through the double doors that led to the back of the emergency room where the patient rooms were. Nurses, doctors, beeping machines, crying children, and a stationed security guard outside of room three greeted them.

"Hold on," Cadence said, stepping in front of Gloria. "You're gonna have to tell me something because this is just too much.”

“I will,” she replied, nodding to the guard. “Soon as Detective Carter gives the okay. Just know I did what I had to do. Jackson was never in any real danger.”

Cadence balked, placing hands on her hips. “Detective Carter was the one who told me you were a dirty cop working for Lester. Now, you’re saying …” Cadence waved her off. “I just want to see my husband.”

“Very well,” Gloria remarked, opening the glass door and pulling the privacy curtain to the side. She remained outside of the room, claiming the spot the guard was in when they arrived.

“Jackson,” Cadence cried, rushing to him and throwing her arms around his chest. “I love you so much.”

“Baby,” he replied, burying his face in her neck, and pulling her more into his body. “All I could think about was getting home to you and Jackie.”

Cadence kissed Jackson’s bruised cheek, giving him a thorough once-over. He had a gauze bandage on the left side of his head.

“What happened here?” she asked, touching the dressing gently.

“It doesn’t matter.” Jackson smiled, wrapping his fingers around her hand, and pulling them to his lips. “The only thing that’s important is that I’m here with you.” He paused, gazing at his beautiful wife.

They were lost in each other’s trance for a moment when Jackson flinched, startling Cadence.

“Have you talked to my mom and dad? Do they know

what's going on?" Jackson asked.

"I spoke with Ella the day you were arrested. She didn't take the news well, and your father did what he could to calm her," Cadence winced, remembering the stress in Ella's voice. "When I learned the truth, I called your dad. Thomas told me not to worry, and then said he would explain everything to mom," she said, retrieving the phone from her purse. "I haven't had a chance to call them today. I rushed straight to the hospital from the courthouse. I needed to lay my eyes on you first to make sure you were okay."

Cadence dialed Jackson's parents, and she handed him the phone when Ella answered. They talked for several minutes with Jackson reassuring his mom every few seconds that he was alright. Everyone in the room remained silent until he ended the call.

"I'm happy to see you, brother-in-law," Crystal said, moving to the opposite side of the bed, squeezing Jackson's leg. "You had us worried for a bit."

"Yea. What she said," Tony cosigned, giving Jackson a fist bump.

"Can you please tell me what happened once, *she* took you?" Cadence asked, pointing at Gloria, who stood in the hall by the doorway.

"Cut her a break, baby," Jackson advised, shifting on the bed. "Things aren't what they seem."

A knock on the glass caught everyone's attention as Gloria opened the door, then stepped aside. Detective Carter and Sly entered the cramped room.

"How are you feeling?" Detective Carter asked, standing at the foot of the bed.

"Much better now," Jackson answered, smiling at his wife.

"You look a hell of a lot better too," Sly commented, sliding his thumbs through the belt loops on his jeans. "How're your feet?"

"What does he mean?" Cadence questioned, looking toward the two lumps under the covers at the foot of the bed.

"I can feel my toes. All of them, thanks to you, Sly."

"Good."

"Where did y'all take Lester?" Jackson asked, narrowing his gaze on Detective Carter.

"He's back in the county jail's infirmary with my partner, Jason Sharpe, standing guard," Detective Carter answered. "He ain't going anywhere."

"Hold on," Cadence exclaimed with a raised voice. "I need to know what the heck happened. Why *that* woman was involved." She frowned, pointing in Gloria's direction. "And how Lester came to be a part of this."

"Breathe easy, Sissy," Crystal soothed. "They're gonna ask us to leave if you don't keep your voice down."

"I need answers. Now."

The room got so quiet that the only sounds heard, came from the monitors, footsteps in the hall, and phones ringing in the distance at the nurse's station.

Detective Carter tapped on the glass, and Gloria entered the room and shut the door.

"Yes."

"It's time for full disclosure," Detective Carter stated. "What I'm about to say effects, everyone, in this room. That includes you."

Cadence had been waiting for this moment. Jackson moved over, and she climbed in next to him. Crystal sat at the foot of the bed, and Sly and Tony stood next to one another. Detective Carter and Gloria had everyone's undivided attention.

"Thanks to Sly and Tony, we learned that Judge Duncan is Lester's uncle," Detective Carter said, leaning against the sink. "And he's responsible for getting Lester out of jail."

"What?" Cadence hollered, covering her mouth.

"I heard Lester mention his Uncle Clark while he held me captive. I wasn't sure if it was the drugs or if I was dreaming."

"*Drugs*," Cadence repeated, glancing up at Jackson.

"I was in and out of consciousness for days," he said, staring at Gloria.

"Who drugged you?"

"I did," Gloria admitted. "It was for his own safety."

"The more you talk …" Cadence shook her head.

Detective Carter snapped his fingers, and the room fell silent. He shot a glance at everyone before he continued. "Judge Clark Duncan is Lester's biological uncle. He visited Lester in the room designated for prisoners to meet with their attorneys the night he was arrested. The correctional officer that escorted Lester to the room is my confidential informant."

"The plan was to say that Lester had been in protective custody when he was actually missing from the jail," Gloria added, stepping forward. "Lester confessed that to me, while

Jackson was sedated. He said that Judge Duncan would have him back in custody once the trial began, pretty much giving him the freedom to do whatever he wanted, then slipping Lester back in lock-up, guaranteeing him an alibi."

"They were using Jackson as a pawn to break me?" Cadence asked.

"Yes," Gloria responded. "I had been infiltrating Lester's drug ring for six months. I got in close with him. Established a relationship. Became his woman."

"Shared his bed?" Crystal smirked.

"Made him believe I was trustworthy," Gloria shot back, narrowing a gaze on Crystal. "When he came up with the plan to get Jackson away from Cadence, I jumped at the opportunity. Who knows how the abduction might have gone down had one of his other associates took Jackson?" Gloria glanced at Cadence. "I had to make it believable. I'm sorry for any grief I've caused you."

Jackson stroked Cadence's arm.

"I borrowed a burner from one of the inmates in exchange for adding money on his books," Tony said, glancing at Detective Carter, who returned an incredulous stare. "I snapped pictures of Judge Duncan and the warden talking in the kitchen after the final count. I didn't know who the judge was at the time, but anytime the warden is having a meeting." Tony lifted his fingers, making air quotes. "In the kitchen—— after hours." He smirked. "I knew nothing about that was kosher."

Cadence couldn't believe the things she was hearing.

"That's when I told Sly about what I'd seen, and showed

him the photos."

"I had made my rounds on Block D where Lester's cell was, but something told me to check again," Sly said, adjusting the eagle medallion on the gold chain around his neck. "When I did, Lester was gone."

"His cellmate didn't say anything?" Cadence asked.

"It doesn't work like that," Sly informed her. "You could beat them within an inch of their life, and ninety-eight percent of the inmates still wouldn't snitch."

"That's the night you called me," Jackson remarked.

Sly nodded. "I'd been on duty watching your house the day Jackson was arrested," he added, angling a glance at Cadence and Jackson. "Something about the exchange outside didn't feel right, so I followed them to an old boarded-up furniture warehouse. I didn't know at the time that Lester was involved."

"But the probability was there, seeing as though he was no longer in jail," Cadence snapped, outraged by the entire situation.

"So, this is where we're at," Detective Carter said, splaying his hands in front of him. "The warden agreed to testify that the judge coerced him into releasing Lester as a way to scare Cadence into not testifying, hopefully resulting in a mistrial for Detective O'Brien since she was the star witness for the prosecution," Detective Carter said, folding his arms across his chest. "In return, the warden gets immunity for his cooperation."

Chapter 26

"Do I have to sit in the hall until Reed calls me back to the stand to finish the cross-examination?" Cadence asked Knox as she, Jackson, Crystal, Gloria, Sly, Tony, and Detective Carter approached the courtroom.

"No," Knox replied. "You will not be retaking the stand."

A huge weight had been lifted from her spirit. Jackson squeezed Cadence's hand and smiled down at her. Cadence found solace in his caring eyes, even though she was worried about him.

"You had no business checking yourself out of the hospital," Cadence scolded as they entered the courtroom, claiming the first bench behind the prosecution table. "I told you I'd be fine."

"Stop fussing and let Jax be the man and husband he's needs to be," Sly chided, nudging Cadence. "You know he wouldn't want to be anywhere else other than beside you—supporting you."

"Mind your business," she teased, slapping his knee.

"He's right," Jackson leaned over and whispered in her ear. "Right here. Next to you. Is where I wanna be."

He's so stubborn. "I love you too."

Cadence glanced over her shoulder just as Detective O'Brien and Reed were walking up the aisle. The sight of him made her stomach lurch. Before she could turn her head, Detective O'Brien locked eyes with her, then winked. Instantly, Cadence's mood changed.

"I can't believe this jerk," Jackson commented, glaring at the back of Detective O'Brien's head.

"You saw that, too," Sly growled through clenched teeth.

"Baby, ignore him," Jackson said to Cadence. "Effing unbelievable."

"All rise. The Honorable Judge Clark Duncan presiding," the bailiff announced.

"Honorable," Cadence whispered, getting to her feet. "That's disputable."

"Please be seated."

"This is the people versus Detective Paul O'Brien," Judge Duncan said, sitting upright like a statue, sliding on his glasses. "Any questions before I bring in the jurors?"

"Yes, Your Honor," Knox said, standing, buttoning his suit jacket, and folding his hands in front of him. "The prosecution would like to put forth a new motion."

"For?"

"We want you to recuse yourself from this case for conflict of interest. It has come to our attention that you are related to Lester James, the known drug kingpin associated with Detective O'Brien's case. In addition to that, we have irrefutable proof that you blackmailed the warden into releasing Lester James from jail on the same night he'd been arrested," Knox stated, scanning the documents before him. "Which resulted in the kidnapping of Jackson Goldsmith, the husband of the prosecution's witness, Cadence Goldsmith."

The spectators in the gallery gasped.

Cadence glanced over at Detective O'Brien and Reed, and the stunned expression on Reed's face was similar to how Cadence felt when she learned of the information. She was convinced that he didn't know anything about it. But Detective O'Brien was a different story. He looked as smug as he'd always did.

Judge Duncan glared at Knox so hard that Cadence thought his eyeballs would pop out of their sockets.

"Really," Judge Duncan said, leaning back in his seat. "Why not mention this on the first day of trial?"

"We only learned of the conflict yesterday after court was adjourned," Knox shot back.

"Do you have any proof of this accusation?"

"Yes, Your Honor," Knox replied, sounding self-assured.

"We have a witness who will testify to the conflict."

"And when can you produce this witness?"

"Right now," Knox fired back; his chin tilted heavenward. "The people call Cook County Jail Warden, Nathan Griggs to the stand."

A synchronized shift in the seats echoed in the courtroom as everyone turned around. The gray-haired man with oily-colorless skin and hardened facial features, probably from years of surmountable stress, came forward.

The chatter from the gallery became louder. Someone called the judge crooked. Another person said this feels like entrapment. A woman's voice shouted, "Finally something that will stick."

Cadence glanced at Jackson, then whispered. "It's much more to this than we knew."

Judge Duncan banged his gavel. "Settle down before I have everyone removed," he warned, looking out toward the gallery. After the noise ceased, Judge Duncan took off his glasses and said in the sourest of tones, "I recuse myself."

Warden Griggs stopped mid-stride.

"Bailiff." A woman in an identical black robe with beautiful salt and pepper, curly-textured hair, emerged from Judge Duncan's chambers. "Cuff him."

Judge Duncan's head whipped in the direction of his colleague. "What happened to professional courtesy? Where's my due process?"

"Who's that?" Cadence whispered to no one in particular.

"Chief Judge, Dorothy Tate," Knox said over his shoulder.

"I met with her late last night."

"Are you questioning my authority?" Judge Tate snapped, interlocking her fingers.

"No, Chief Judge Tate," he coward.

"Damn." Sly nodded, crossing one leg over the other. "Now, that's power."

"Detective O'Brien, your bond has been revoked," Judge Tate announced, as the bailiff placed handcuffs on Judge Duncan. "Mr. Reed, please advise your client on what happens when he breaks the law while awaiting trial. He should already know, but apparently, he needs a reminder."

The corners of Cadence's mouth lifted, resulting in a full smile that made her cheeks hurt.

"Sheriff," Judge Tate called out, and two men came forward. One stood in front of Detective O'Brien, pulling his hands forward while putting cuffs on his wrists, while the other stood alongside him. "A new judge will be appointed to this case. Until then, court is adjourned."

"I know this prolongs the case," Knox said, turning to Cadence, still holding the documents in his hands.

"But it feels like a win," she countered, smiling at Knox. "Lester's off the streets, and now, so is Detective O'Brien."

"We don't have to be on guard constantly," Jackson added, kissing Cadence on the temple.

The stress and anxiety that had been accompanying Cadence daily had lifted some. Before she felt like justice wouldn't be served, she now could see the possibilities.

"You should've died in that accident," Detective O'Brien

spat over the sheriff's shoulder. "Your lucks running out."

"What did you say?" Cadence shouted, pulling away from Jackson.

"Did you just threaten my client?" Knox barked, throwing the documents in his hand on the table.

"What are you doing?" Reed asked through gritted teeth. "Be quiet."

Cadence flashed back to the accident. Everything was a blur after the impact. Her body felt heavy and wet. She heard voices. One man. One woman. No… two men.

She squeezed her eyelids shut.

You're not supposed to move them. You can cause more damage. Wait for the paramedics.

"It. Was. You," Cadence growled, opening her eyes and pointing at Detective O'Brien.

He grinned, then maneuvered, knocking the sheriff on the side of him off balance while yanking the other sheriff's service weapon from its holster. Detective O'Brien angled the gun in Cadence's direction, but before he could pull the trigger, four shots whizzed past Cadence's head, hitting Detective O'Brien center mass.

The people in the gallery screamed as they ducked behind the benches and fled the courtroom. The cops in the gallery drew their weapons and stood their ground until they realized who fired the shots.

Cadence tasted the Sulphur from the gun smoke. Her body trembled, and her ears wrung from the close proximity of the gunfire. She'd take a little hearing loss in exchange for her life.

"Somebody call an ambulance," Detective Carter order, hopping over the divider with his weapon still drawn, approaching Detective O'Brien.

Reed fell to his knees, pressing his index and middle fingers into the groove of Detective O'Brien's neck to the side of his windpipe. He sighed, dropping his chin to his chest. "He's gone."

Cadence stared, gripping the back of the bench.

"Baby, you okay?" Jackson asked, wrapping his arms around her waist.

"I'm good," Cadence replied, sliding her hand over his. "I say justice was served."

Epilogue

One year had passed since the mayhem of Detective O'Brien's trial, and Cadence and her family couldn't have been happier. The fact that yesterday, Lester was sentenced to twenty years in prison for Braelyn's murder, and serving a consecutive twenty years for kidnapping Jackson, on top of the pending investigation for the five bodies found on the gun, had sweetened the return to normal life.

"Thanks for letting the kids spend the night," Steven commented, bringing in two cases of wine and beer.

"I hope they weren't much trouble," Deb added, crossing her fingers.

"None at all," Cadence replied, swooping down to catch Caden, who was wobbling by on those fast toddler feet. "He loved having kids here closer to his age and size."

"I bet he did," Steven remarked, making silly faces at Caden. "I think it's cool that you're throwing this party."

"It's finally our time to celebrate," Cadence said, hiking Caden up on her hip while he played in her hair. "This may sound strange, but in hindsight, I'm glad Caden wasn't home during Detective O'Brien's trial while we endured all that craziness."

"Me too," Jackson said, walking over. He pinched Caden's tiny nose, then relieved Steven of one of the cases. "The NICU was the best place for him from a security standpoint."

"Liquid courage," Knox teased, walking through the front door, pointing to the alcohol in Jackson and Steven's arms.

"Hey, Knox," Cadence greeted. "I'm glad you could make it."

"I wouldn't have missed it. We've earned this celebration," Knox replied, taking Caden out of her arms. "And it's time that you start calling me Aaron. We're way past formalities."

"Gotcha, *Aaron*." She laughed, throwing her head back.

"That goes for me, too," Detective Carter chimed in, stepping around Aaron with a beautiful woman on his arm. "This is my wife, Patricia."

"Nice to meet you," Cadence smiled, giving her a hug. "You guys are always welcomed to our home. I will forever be indebted to your husband."

"That's my Xavier," Patricia beamed, taking off her ankle-length fur coat. Xavier took the garment and laid it over his arm.

"I'll put that up for you," Cadence said, retrieving the coat. She went into her bedroom, laid the fur on the bed with the other guest's outerwear, then returned to the living room. "You fellas make yourself at home. Thomas has the football game on in the media room, and my momma and Ella are taking bets."

"Say what?" Xavier leaned back.

"Oh yea," Jackson countered, signaling Aaron, Steven, and Xavier to follow him with a tilt of the head. "Them mama's ain't no joke. Phylicia will take all of your money while Ella's plying you with homemade finger foods and drinks."

"Sounds like a good time." Aaron chuckled, handing Caden back to Cadence. "I'm in."

The men disappeared to the rear of the house, dodging three little people, and Crystal as she chased the kids, nearly knocking Cadence into the wall. Caden wiggled his way down her leg, trying to catch his sister, cousins, and auntie.

Cadence inhaled, taking in the harmonious love, laughter, joy, and new friends in her home. She couldn't be more grateful for the blessings that surrounded her.

"Thank you, God, for sparing my life and making it fuller and richer than before."

If you haven't already, read ***Sugarcoated Deception, Book 1 of the Deception Series***, and take the journey with Cadence and Jackson to see the obstacles they overcame to get to this point in their lives. You won't be disappointed. If you want to know more about **Detective Xavier Carter** and his unconventional lifestyle with not one, but two wives, check out ***The Husband We Share***.

Both excerpts follow the story. Happy reading!

Sugarcoated Deception

(Deception Series Book 1)

Four words would put an end to Cadence Goldsmith's perfect life.

"That's Mr. Goldsmith, Mommy."

She searched out the source of that small childlike screech, an unnatural occurrence in the Adali Global Reveal. The event was an exclusive affair for people who worked in the European auto market.

Cadence peered around the velvet curtain from her spot backstage of the McCormick Place Convention Center, surprised to find that her husband, Jackson, and mother, Phylicia were sitting in the front row next to a scowling Steven Bekker, her work nemesis.

"Hiiiiiii, Mr. Goldsmith," a little girl with light-brown skin, blue-eyes and puffy blonde twists crooned, as she rushed to stand near her husband. "You work at my school."

Cadence grimaced. Why was a child there and why was she so interested in Jackson? Wait, was that an image of her husband on that child's shirt? She almost couldn't make it out because the girl's fist twisted the material.

"I present to you, CDO, Cadence Goldsmith."

Applause rang out as she strutted center stage with her attention on the bleached-blonde woman wearing a navy dress, who grinned and winked at her before taking an empty seat next to Jackson and pulling the little girl onto her lap. Jackson glanced at Cadence, then frowned as he put his focus back on the woman. She didn't miss the panic that took over his features for a split second.

Cadence's heart surged with a bit of panic of her own. She prayed that her confidence would still show through, even though relishing the acknowledgement of being the designer of the first self-driving automobile was taking a back seat to Jackson and the unknown guests.

Jackson, who seemed occupied with the distraction that little girl had become, hadn't acknowledged Cadence at all. He and the woman were having a heated, but whispered conversation. Jackson's body language—tense and angry—screamed discomfort.

"May I have everyone's attention please," Cadence said walking to the edge of the stage, standing in front of her husband.

Jackson's brown eyes gazed into hers, but the comfort and security she usually felt was missing.

"Mommy, now," the little girl asked.

"Shhhh." The woman placed an index finger to her thin pink lips. "Not yet."

Cadence raised an eyebrow, then glanced at her husband.

The lights dimmed, and Cadence began the PowerPoint presentation of the newest addition to the Adali luxury car fleet.

Ten minutes later, every person, except for Steven and the mystery woman, were on their feet clapping.

Mike lifted a hand to settle the crowd. "Cadence Goldsmith has a bright future with Adali, and we, along with the two most important people in her life, would like to present her with the Outstanding Innovative Design Award."

"Yay, Mr. Goldsmith," the little girl squealed, slapping her hands together. Cadence's attention was drawn to the child whose eyes matched the woman she assumed to be her mother. High heels clicking across the stage accompanied by Jackson's signature fragrance snapped Cadence from the trance.

Mike handed a plaque with the Adali emblem engraved on it to Cadence.

"Thank you." She shook his hand trying to play it cool even though she wanted to shatter the surrounding windows with a high-pitched scream.

"Congratulations." Jackson beamed with cautionary excitement written all over his face as he embraced his wife.

"Who the hell is that woman," she whispered through a clenched-teeth grin as her lips brushed the side of his ear.

Jackson's dark-skin ashen. "Her name's Braelyn," he replied, planting a timid kiss on her cheek. "We'll talk later."

Her mother stepped forward. "Your father would be so proud of you."

Small feet galloping up the stairs onto the stage made everyone in the audience gasp. Cadence peered over Phylicia's shoulder at the lively little girl sprinting forward, spotting a picture of Jackson splayed on the front of her shirt.

Executive's plucked phones from their purses and suit jacket pockets.

Security rushed in. "We're going to have to ask you to get your child and leave, ma'am."

"I have a right to be here," Braelyn exclaimed, throwing a glance at Steven as she flashed the VIP badge.

After a thorough inspection, the guard said with a remorseful tone, "My apologies, Ms. Nevels." He glanced at Mike. "She has clearance."

"Nevels," Cadence whispered, wondering why that name sounded so familiar.

"Show everyone your cute shirt, Jackie," Braelyn instructed, smiling at the pretty girl, before planting a menacing glare at Cadence and Jackson.

Jackie spread her arms wide, facing the audience. "Look, Mommy." She pointed jumping in place. Everybody's taking my picture." She put her hands on her hips and said, "Cheeeeese."

The lump in Cadence's throat grew larger with every word she read on the back of Jackie's shirt.

Jackson Goldsmith Is My Daddy.

AVAILABLE ON AMAZON
https://bit.ly/sugarcoateddeception

The Husband We Share

Lauren Carter screamed and bolted upright in her bed, snatched from the reoccurring nightmare that had plagued her for years. She touched a finger to her right ear, expecting to feel a drop of blood, but found none. Damp tendrils of hair clung to her flushed face as she swiped a hand to move them to clear her vision.

"Help me please!"

That voice then, and now, still echoed in Lauren's mind along with the consequences of Lauren's mistake. Hours went by as Lauren was forced to listen to Shawn's shrieks of pain. Trapped on the other side of the door, Lauren was powerless to save the little girl who had come to depend on her for so much.

"You'd better stop screaming, or I'll kill you," a raspy voice had barked. A voice belonging to a complete stranger; a man who'd managed to sneak in through the back door of the Community Center, then hide inside the building and lay in wait for the right time to...

The twelve-year-old girl who cried out for Lauren's help had barely survived a horrific experience that would dismantle someone who didn't have the support it took to heal. Shawn had managed to piece her life back together. Unfortunately, Lauren still felt the aftereffects.

Disoriented from the recurring nightmare, a chill from the

master bedroom rendered Lauren numb. A red lace gown clung to her petite frame, wet from the perspiration that peppered her golden skin. She wrapped trembling arms about her midriff, but they provided no comfort. Lauren had watched Shawn's ordeal in excruciating detail through the sliver pane of glass the steel door offered.

"Help me," the girl screamed, but the man wrapped his thick fingers around her throat cutting off any further speech.

This time in her nightmare, tornado sirens had roared loud enough to shatter glass windows and pierce eardrums. A howling wind swept through the building as the steel bars finally receded, and the evil man disappeared, leaving a world of sadness and torment behind.

Lauren scanned the dark bedroom, panting as her heart hammered against her chest causing an ache that wouldn't subside anytime soon. The guilt threatened to swallow her whole. She had allowed fear of someone else to control her actions, making her less mindful of following proper procedures. Now, thirteen years later, she sat on her bed reliving an experience that had been all consuming to the point she had been forced to seek medical help.

She lowered her head, then took several deep breaths, watching her chest slowly rise and fall in efforts to create a steady breathing pattern.

Though the siren in her dream had silenced when she opened her eyes, some type of siren was still going strong on this side of Lauren's waking nightmare.

"What is that noise?" she whispered, and her voice seemed

to disappear into corners of the master bedroom.

She focused on the digital clock on the nightstand, then shifted from the warmth under the comforter, her heart hammering in her chest all over again. When she stepped a few feet, the chilling grip of the dream loosened, and the cause for the blaring sound became that much clearer in her mind. At nearly three in the morning someone's car alarm was wailing louder than a Jessye Norman opera performance.

Lauren shivered as another chill raced through her body the moment her feet absorbed the coolness of the mahogany floor. Snatching a red satin robe from its home on the arm of a pewter suede wingback chair, she wrapped it around her body before rushing down the winding staircase and straight to the living room window. By the time she peered out of the vertical blinds, a few answering chirps had caused the noise to come to a complete stop.

She let out a heavy sigh, realizing that sleep wouldn't revisit her so soon after such an adrenaline rush. Normally the pills would keep her in a restful state through the entire night— no matter what happened in this corner of the world.

So, what's different this time?

Something was off, and her subconscious finally registered a particular issue with startling clarity. Xavier. Why didn't she wake him before venturing down to check things out for herself? Why hadn't he comforted her when she woke up shrieking from a horror that no longer existed?

The empty feel of the Tudor home they owned on the south side of Chicago, in the Beverly neighborhood, enveloped her like several layers of fog descending over Lake Michigan. Her husband's Cadillac Escalade wasn't in the driveway parked next to the White Lexus truck he'd bought her as a "just because" gift when she had been named as one of Chicago's Leading Hair Stylists in Essence Magazine.

She tried to shake off the feeling of melancholy which settled in as she made her way through the dark house, thinking that maybe she somehow misinterpreted things.

"Oh my Lord," she whispered as a shocking reality set in. "Maybe that alarm was from his truck, and the damn thieves got away with it."

That had to be the only explanation for him to be missing in action. Since more DEA agents had been sent to Chicago, undercover work by local police was at a minimum. Xavier would have told Lauren of any new assignments.

Lauren climbed the stairs to the upper level, ran the length of the hallway, passing a red bamboo floor vase and causing it to shake from her efforts.

"Xavier! Xavier, wake up," Lauren yelled, bursting into the master bedroom. She flipped the light switch and froze; placing her hands on hips that her husband said would cause a blind man to regain his sight and dance a grateful jig. Evidently, that blind man had a better chance of seeing them right now than her husband would.

"Where the hell is he?"

Lauren's gaze swept the area, taking in the king-sized black canopy poster bed with two sheer drapes cascading down evenly on both sides. Then her fingers tipped the dimmer. Her eyesight quickly adjusted to the bright light illuminating a room designed in shades of ruby red and Charleston gray—colors that spoke to a blend of the couple's taste.

Only Lauren's side of the bed showed signs of recent use. Xavier's was as silky smooth, just as it had been the morning before. Even the scent of Edge Shave gel was barely discernable.

She massaged her temples, allowing several scenarios to run through her mind. Her husband, a Narc with the Chicago Police Department, had been involved with the kind of cases that put him in the same vicinity with high-level drug dealers, managing confidential informants, and the type of surveillance that had made his career a sometimes-dangerous engagement. Nothing she was aware of would cause him to disappear without a word. And he certainly hadn't seemed worried about anything earlier that evening. Her body tingled with the sweet memories.

Xavier had touched, teased, and tongued every part of her soul along with every inch of her buttercream skin in the shower just hours ago. Her body had trembled and convulsed, as he drove her to the point that was completely out of control. He had perfected the craft of making Lauren experience the ultimate orgasmic euphoria. Their lovemaking now was as good as their wedding night had been a little over nine years ago. Only better. Coupled with the fact that he was also loving, caring, and an excellent provider, made her the happiest woman on the south side of Chicago, if not the world.

A smile crept across her face remembering that afterward,

they had spooned and fell asleep in each other's arms. She ran her fingers through wavy shoulder-length hair, frowning as she tried to recall a fuzzier time, thinking; I thought that's what happened?

The smile disappeared the moment she tried putting the pieces together, and something didn't fit. Needless to say, no matter how much sleep was lacking and how much she needed to be on point to do an early morning favor for a last-minute client, she was too wired to put her head back on the pillow.

Lauren Carter wasn't sure if she should be pissed off at Xavier for being left alone or concerned because he wasn't in the place he was supposed to be.

"Where the hell is my husband?"

AVAILABLE ON AMAZON
https://bit.ly/thehusbandweshare

Also by London St. Charles

STANDALONES

The Husband We Share

Betrayal of Trust

King of Chatham

ANTHOLOGIES

Sugar

Just One Kiss

CASTLE SERIES

Kings of the Castle (collaboration, not an anthology)

DECEPTION SERIES

Sugarcoated Deception

Deadly Deception